Praise for

On *The l*

"Her following will grow immensely with this novel."
Woman's Way

"Quirky and humorous."
Cork Examiner

On *The Pineapple Tart*

"This book is sheer bliss."
The Sunday World

"Funny, tender-hearted, immensely satisfying."
Woman's Way

On *A Soft Touch*

"A gloriously entertaining tale . . . it's a definite must."
The Sunday World

On *Kissing the Frog*

"It is extremely funny . . . "
The Star

Anne Dunlop

Dolly Holiday

The DOLLY HOLIDAY

The DOLLY HOLIDAY

ANNE DUNLOP

POOLBEG

First published 1993
by Poolbeg Press Ltd
123 Baldoyle Industrial Estate
Dublin 13, Ireland
Paperback edition 1994

Reprinted August 1995
Reprinted December 1996

A catalogue record for this book is available from the British Library.

ISBN 1 85371 325 2

Cover illustration by Wendy Robinson
Cover design by Poolbeg Group Services Ltd
Printed by The Guernsey Press Ltd,
Vale, Guernsey, Channel Islands.

The Publishers gratefully acknowledge the support of

The Arts Council / An Chomhairle Ealaíon

and the Arts Council of Northern Ireland

About the Author

Anne Dunlop was born in Castledawson, Co Derry, Northern Ireland in 1968. She graduated in Agricultural Science at UCD. Anne Dunlop now works as an air stewardess for Gulf Air. She has four novels published by Poolbeg.

Also by Anne Dunlop

The Pineapple Tart
A Soft Touch
Kissing the Frog

Published by Poolbeg

For Helen and Winston

CHAPTER ONE

"I'm not looking at anyone in particular," said Mummy as Daisy and I came into the kitchen, "but did you know that in the first year of having sex women should have a smear test done?"

Mummy says this is a biological fact and she learnt it at her Biology O Level Night Classes. Daddy is right about education ruining women. Last week he got off the tractor looking for a hand with some sheep he was moving.

"Can't, darling, I've got a test tonight and I don't know what an enzyme is."

There is something very innocent about such parents. That's why we continue living with them, Daisy and me. I can't conduct myself with normal people now.

Daisy blushed when Mummy said "sex". Daisy is a big healthy girl who pulls calves and talks about bulling and tupping to Daddy. But she is very modest about immoral relationships. She tried to have one once with Johnboy Jackson but it was a disaster and she ran away and hid herself for months afterwards. She's half innocent too, a million brain cells and not an ounce of common sense, but we tell people she is artistic to take the bad look off it.

I ran away with her, because I have no sense and we went to Kinelvin where my sister Jennifer lives.

Jennifer is a wicked Jezebel but she got married before

anybody guessed and her husband is a gentleman of impeccable pedigree and civilised temperament. He's really good-looking too. No one knows what he sees in Jennifer who rarely washes and is so unsuitable. Of course she's very horsy, and rides like a Hun and she produced a son within the first nine months of marriage. She was talking to me on the telephone at the time.

Richard was at Kinelvin, Richard Knight. I used to know him at university. He was in my class. He is engaged to a friend of ours, Elisabeth Churchill-Knox. They were always very fond of each other. I am very happy for them. Elisabeth is very golden and very suitable.

I met Elisabeth in Dublin in the summertime, but it wasn't a success. My man Huge behaved very badly. Huge proposed to me once. We were in bed together and he said, "You're mad about me. Let's get married," but I pretended I didn't hear him and he never asked me again.

Sarah, my most bossy sister, says you should expect a man to ask you five times before accepting. Sarah has an attitude problem about men and she calls it Feminism. I said that wearing dungarees and Doc Martens didn't stop a girl getting raped. She said that everyone knew Huge blacked my eye in Dublin and no doubt I deserved it. But then Sarah thinks God is a woman.

She scolded Mummy for saying "smear test" and scolded Laura for laughing. Laura, my big sister in more ways than one, has retained her adolescent fascination with smutty language through marriage, desertion and motherhood. "I'm built for speed not comfort" is her expression of the moment. Should the opportunity present itself I privately believe she would run a mile. Since "the Yank" she has interfered with no one. She says "the Yank" was all biology and no chemistry. Quoting The Book I tell her an empty vessel makes the most noise.

It is unhealthy to live at Derryrose. Mummy and Daddy are escaping to a brown and white bungalow at the bottom of the garden, once they rob us of enough rent to pay for it. The novelty of Mummy's new job has worn off her already.

"I haven't spoken a word to any of them in two days." She was constructing a shopping list, scanning the office, sulky. "They're all going on holidays."

"Not sausages again", I protested, "we've had sausages three days in a row."

"Your father and Laura won't eat anything else. Your father doesn't like chicken nuggets or gammon steaks."

"Laura will eat anything that's processed."

Everyone helps to pay for the brown and white bungalow. The sooner it's built the sooner they move.

No matter how often Daisy got on and off the new electronic digital bathroom scales they remained at ten stone thirteen pounds. Sarah had saved her petrol stamps for months to buy the scales and we were all weighing in to try them out.

"Cut your hair and shave your legs," I suggested, she was already in the nip.

"It's all right for you," said Daisy, covering her modesty with Laura's yellow velvet dressing gown and trying not to watch while I stripped, "I bet you wouldn't weigh ten stone with a lamb under each arm."

"Probably not," I agreed, jumping off so she wouldn't see and be depressed, "but I'm sure that big bag of salted peanuts you ate in Wellworths earlier didn't help."

Johnboy Jackson, a brave man and a glutton for punishment, is the love of Daisy's life. Still, he took off to the Costa Brava about a week ago on a cheap cancellation holiday with Willie Simpson and Daisy has been comfort eating ever since. As we speak Johnboy is probably riding a moped around the nudist beach, himself and Willie Simpson. Drink and women are the ruination of decent men.

The grass is green, the sky is blue and Willie Simpson is a halfwit. We used to have this joke that Willie Simpson went to Special Care School. Because one time the police caught him drunk in charge of his bicycle and summonsed him and made him do his cycling proficiency test outside the Leisure Centre where everybody saw him. Willie thought the whole thing was a tremendous joke and gave everyone the fingers when he was finished. He's more eccentric than mad.

"I feel like an empty box without Johnboy," Daisy moaned, "no matter how many nuts I eat."

Being a bit empty of action myself since Huge, I took her to The Cobbled Courtyard on Saturday night to flirt and forget. Sarah wouldn't come with us because she says The Cobbled Courtyard is a meat market and an insult to intelligent females. Sarah stopped preaching her Feminist Gospel to us the day Laura suggested feminists had taken the balls out of sex. She has been reduced to revelling in a Martyr For The Cause Act and tiresomely practising what she preaches.

Daisy and I entered The Buxom Wench Personality and Beauty Competition for a laugh. All the Wenches danced to *Do You Want To Funk* and we were both chosen from the heaving sea of funking wenches. Daisy told the judges she was a Captain in the Girls' Brigade, I told them I was a stripper, but neither of us qualified for the finals.

When she got home Daisy ate half a packet of Hobnob biscuits sandwiched together with cheese, and worried about telling that lie about the Girls' Brigade.

I did the Joan Collins Workout, with Stretch and Seal around my waist to sweat off the fat faster, and wished I had worn fake tan. All the other contestants had mahogany legs. Our evening out had not been a success. Sarah, smirking, said, "I told you so" the next morning.

Daisy keeps looking in jewellery shop windows at diamond rings and is presently suffering Engagement Ring Blues. It's not that Johnboy has never proposed, Daisy considers that a formality, but it is finding The Ring that is causing problems. She says she knows what type of ring she wants, there is a photograph of it on the back of a bridal magazine we bought when Laura got married. It doesn't bother Daisy that the crusher in the photograph probably costs £40,000 and she will not be offered one a fortieth of the price. Her grievances are concentrated around the provincial town selection.

Daddy is quoted as saying Smyth's of Magherafelt is the jewellery centre of the universe so in we went to confirm what we had already suspected. It was Belfast or nowhere.

I borrowed Great Aunt Maisie's 1942 Chanel suit and went with Daisy on the bus to Belfast. Sarah wouldn't come. She thinks engagement rings are a symbol of Female Oppression. I think Sarah has forgotten how to laugh.

We chose to hit Wallace because that was where Johnboy's sister, Sandra "The Rabbit" Flemming, got her ring, and she's married to the son of a millionaire. Daisy, dressed in Mummy's fur, told the shopgirl, "I think it's so much wiser to have an idea of what I suit before Sir John comes in to buy," as she fitted on every diamond in the shop. The one we settled for cost £13,500, but as Daisy said the whole thing was hypothetical so she might as well have extravagant tastes.

I have also been helping her construct a wedding list. Hundred pound notes was the last thing we put on it. And this weight obsession is to fit into Mummy's size 12 wedding dress. What Johnboy doesn't know won't hurt him. Daisy's looking for a house for them to live in.

Daisy's romance is good to share because I have no man myself. I exist in a limbo of pleasant nothingness. I could be like this for the rest of my life and it would be easy. Pleasant nothingness.

I told her that the only way to lose weight was to stop eating. That was after I reminded her that Johnboy likes a woman he can hold onto. We watched a skinny Margot Fonteyn on the television while Laura grumbled, Daddy slept and Mummy read "Sex Romps in an Attic" out of the tabloid newspaper she was lighting the fire with.

Daisy had Johnboy's homecoming beautifully planned. She was going to be pretty and bubbly and fun. She was not going to fall on him weeping and then examine him under a microscope. She dampened her hair to give it a bit of a curl. Her lipstick matched the colour of her sweater. She bought herself a pair of size 14 jeans which squashed her tummy and were so tight her legs couldn't rub together when she walked. Daisy told Mummy they were not tight, they were just close-fitting.

Johnboy was brown and Willie Simpson was red as fire. He said he had hoped the freckles would join. I chatted to Willie because Johnboy and Daisy were ignoring me, too busy gazing into each other's eyes. Willie said he thought them rather sick-making. Kate's was crowded and hot and Willie stripped to his vest in front of everyone. It was not a real vest, but one of those fashionable T-shirt ones, and it said "Proud to be a Protestant" on the front of it. As he wasn't embarrassed neither was I. I told him he looked healthy.

Cleaning his fingernails with a penknife he informed me that 95% of the wrinkles on the face are caused by the sun. He and Johnboy had been very careful to use sunblock in the Costa Brava. He came back from the bar scolding.

"Women are demanding everything these days, chivalry and going through doors first. It's not fair. I just fought my way through a dozen of them to get a drink, and then I had to let one of them go before me. I'm a believer in Survival of the Fittest myself."

"Hesitancy is bad in a man," he added and put his arm around me. I don't think anyone noticed. "I always thought you Gordons were snobby bitches, but Johnboy says you are misunderstood."

When we got home Mummy asked, "Well Daisy, are you and Johnboy still dating?"

Surprised, Daisy said, "Yes, why wouldn't we be?" which wasn't cheeky but Mummy seemed to think it was and she threw a wobbly and swung a punch at Daisy which fortunately missed. We all think Mummy should stop work. No one is making her go.

Daisy's bedroom walls are plastered with posters of Marilyn Monroe and no less than five framed magazine cut-outs of a man and a woman wrapped round each other in raunchy poses.

"Such sinners," Daisy sighed enviously, handing me a photograph of herself from about fifteen years ago. "Pre-puberty I was such a pretty child, don't you think?"

"You are still pretty," I consoled her but she wasn't convinced. Love makes Daisy insecure. "I wish I didn't enjoy food so much," she said.

Sarah says Daisy retards women's progress because she is so knick knacky.

Chapter Two

Holidaying has gone to Johnboy's head. I think he got too many baked beans with his breakfast fry in the Costa Brava. He brought us over a portable barbecue the day after the "Welcome Home" drink and though it was raining Daisy stood outside with an umbrella over her head and cooked burgers and sausages on it.

Johnboy says the Costa Brava was full of the Fish And Chip Crowd From England but that was OK because he likes fish and chips. My suspicions from last night have been confirmed. He is growing a moustache. Daisy of course thinks this is magnificent and told him he looked "sleazy and sexy", which is to be taken as a compliment. I think it fortunate that her hormones won't allow it or she would probably grow one too to keep him company. I was lying in the bath listening to them outside and reading *The Valley of the Squinting Windows* when he shouted up to me through the open window, "Willie says his dad will lend us the campervan for a week, Helen, you and me and Daisy."

When I got out of the bath Johnboy, who must have still been looking up, said, "You're getting skinny, Helen. I can hardly see your breasts. Have you caught a disease or something?"

"I'm suffering from low self-esteem," I shouted back, "I've caught depression."

"You can't catch depression," said Johnboy firmly.

Daisy said, "I woke this morning and there was a voice in my head shouting 'Fatty' at me, and I couldn't get out of bed because I felt like a plum pudding."

Daisy and Johnboy were both smoking which is called making a statement in the North. Daisy, who can smoke legally when Mummy allows her, was telling him about Bunty, the pup she bought me when my last dog died.

Bunty and Daisy and I had been in Magherafelt cashing our dole cheques and we got stopped by the police on the road home. I opened the door to talk to the policeman because the window doesn't wind down. Bunty leaps from my knee and begins to savage the policeman's trousers. And the policeman says he's going to book me because my dog isn't wearing a seat belt.

Johnboy was so impressed he gave Bunty two of the barbecued garlic sausages. Bunty has become such a raving queen she licks the honey off bread, but screws her nose up at dog food. I even tried her once with Gourmet Doggie Dinners but she screwed her nose up at them too so we gave them to Johnboy's sister the last time she visited and told her it was pâté.

"Helen?" It was Laura, yelling out of an upstairs window.

"Helen, it's an emergency, come quickly." Laura can't come out in the rain because her bedroom slippers are my size 4's that she cut holes in to fit her size 7 feet. Laura has feet like boats. She says they are fitted to her child-bearing hips.

I dashed up stairs to find Laura pointing at week-old dog poo on the hall landing.

"Your dog excreted there."

She watched while I cleaned it up but didn't help. She had just washed her hands, she said. I felt like drop-kicking Bunty twenty yards.

Laura, who hates having the dogs indoors, said last night she dreamed I bought two Charolais bull calves and insisted on having them in the house as well.

That evening Tom Johnston, the most persistent bungalow builder in Ulster, came looking for his money again. Mummy and Daddy hid in the attic above the kitchen so they could hear what he talked to me about. Tom sat in the kitchen with Bunty and me. While Bunty ate his shoe he informed me that the only other Jack Russell to have the same markings as her belonged to Major Ronnie Ferguson. Perhaps, he suggested, they could be sisters?

Finally his persistence crumbled, he tired of waiting for my parents, he went home. I found another dog poo, fresh as grass, under the chair he was sitting on. And I had thought the smell was coming from him.

We had another television argument. Daddy wanted to see how they turned people into werewolves in the movies and Mummy and I wanted to watch *Top Gun*. Mummy thought the men were all deformed in *Top Gun* because they were body builders and their chests were really big.

Sarah's Martyr Act was playing up badly that evening so instead of televising with us she stood in the kitchen baking a cake for Johnboy's sister who is having us round for a barbecue tomorrow night. The last time we were there we were bombarded with the wedding video. Johnboy says that this time it will be the wedding photographs. Visiting Sandra Flemming gives new meaning to the term "captive audience". The wedding video was quite exciting because Mummy features a lot in the church scene. She is obsessed with seeing herself in the movies and isn't modest about pushing herself forward. And the cameraman must have fancied Daisy because he tailed her at the reception.

Usually we take a bottle of homemade wine if we are going anywhere but the Flemmings (junior) are teetotal and homebrew would blow the socks off you. I suggested that we buy a cake, knowing full well that baking one was bound to be a disaster but Sarah Scrooge, the meanest sister in the west, said it would be a waste of money. Sarah has thousands of pounds in her Savings Account and she would fight you for a potato waffle.

Mummy arrived at Flemmings' barbecue with £2,700 in her handbag, to pay the heater man the next day. Mummy has no problem finding money for fitted kitchens and central heating in her bungalow but she won't pay Tom Johnston because she says he will only drink it.

"Derryrose could be burgled," she explained. She had thought of hiding the money in a hockey bag at the back of the Big Attic but the risk of not being able to find it again was greater than the fear of having it stolen.

In the "Young Couple with a Mortgage and Two Cars" class the Flemmings are in a league of their own. No toyhouse in expensive suburbia for them. The Flemmings have acres of garden. Willie Simpson swears that Holy Ian Flemming (lay preacher, accountant, partner in the family's Fitted Bathroom empire) was war-dancing on the lawn in his underpants the morning the Simpsons' bullocks stampeded through it. I'm sure Willie was exaggerating about the language Ian used. The Flemmings are with God.

Sandra "The Rabbit" Flemming name-dropped that she was wearing Benetton leggings and served the barbecue on china dinner plates. The mushroom vol-au-vents tasted strongly of condensed mushroom soup. Sandra stressed that she hadn't made them. She kept saying, "Marigold insisted she make some when she heard I was having a party." Marigold is her mother-in-law. Mummy's false tooth at the front fell out when she bit into the garlic bread but she remembered to hand me the money bag before dashing to the bathroom to stick it back in again.

To her mortification Sandra dashed after her.

"If it's not too much bother, Mrs Gordon," in a tone which suggested that it had better not be too much bother, "could you take your shoes off before you go into the upstairs bathroom? The white mat in front of the washbasin has a rubber back and continuous washing is flaking it away."

Mummy nodded dumbly, frightened to open her mouth in case another tooth fell out.

Sandra raved and raved about the mineral water that we brought with us. No one had the heart to tell her it was gin and tonic in a mineral water bottle.

And, rather obviously, she was sitting in all her wedding photographs to conceal the fact she is half a foot taller than Ian. To make conversation, as we flicked through the album ("The photographer had to have a deposit of £800 before he took a single photograph" – and not one of them of a Gordon!) we told her about the proposed campervan holiday. At first she feigned polite interest (she would not be seen dead in a campervan) but she became really interested when we told her it was Willie's camper and Daisy and I were going unchaperoned with Willie and Johnboy.

To repay the visit (as quickly as was well mannered) we suggested that Sandra and Ian come to the Pictures with us some night. We hoped she would decline, she has been quoted as saying that only gather-ups go to the Pictures, but she was delighted and fixed the night. You got the impression she didn't receive many invitations.

Next day the new Stanley cooker was installed in the brown and white bungalow and I had to sit all day in front of it in case there was some condensation which I had to wipe off in case it stained the mud brown colour. Mummy was painting skirting boards and nagging because Johnboy's mother had phoned and invited her over for afternoon tea to talk about the proposed holiday in the camper van and about Johnboy, Willie, Daisy and me. Eva and Sandra are afraid Johnboy will be "compromising his reputation" going on holiday with us. Mummy doesn't want to have to dress up and talk nicely to Eva. I suggested she take with her a magazine article I read recently, *Have You Had Too Many Lovers?* or even *The Valley of the Squinting Windows* if Eva or Sandra would have the stamina to read it.

Because they don't drink and don't frequent pubs we thought it best to come home for a feed after the Pictures. I don't think the Flemmings realised that everyone was buying their own and we were going to the Chinese. Sandra, bless her, brought us a chunk of wedding cake and a tart from her new deep freeze. I stuck the tart in the lower oven of the range to defrost it. The Chinese idea was better than any dinner party I could have taken two days preparing for.

But when I came out of the dining room and into the kitchen to get the tart I found Bunty had dragged it from the oven and had eaten most of the crust. Soldiering on I served it up anyway with thick lumpy custard as an accompaniment, to hide the bite marks.

"Thanks for the apple tart," said Daisy as they were leaving, though privately we had agreed it was over-sweet.

"Pineapple, Daisy," Sandra corrected, "Pineapple Tart."

"Sometimes," said Johnboy, "I would like to slap my sister's face," but he cheered up when I told him about Bunty savaging the pineapple tart.

Mummy returned from Eva's house in orbit. Eva doesn't approve of the holiday in the campervan. It would be OK, she says, if Daisy and Johnboy were engaged. Apparently it's OK to do lots of naughty things when you are engaged. You can shift other men even, if you want. And if you break your engagement everybody feels sorry for you. If you haven't managed to get his ring on your finger then you have got all you deserve.

And Eva also said to my mother, "I heard Daisy saying 'Shit' on the way out of church on Sunday. That's not very nice language for a young lady, Jennifer. You would never hear Princess Diana saying 'Shit'."

"Mummy, I'm mad to have him marry me," said Daisy pathetically, "but he says that though I'm kind and pleasant to be around I haven't got a tight enough grip on reality to be married to anyone."

"He said that?" said Mummy.

"He says he would get tired of finding soap in the fridge and milk bottles in the bath."

Mummy, being Mummy, told her she would have to change her tactics or change her man, "Those plastic sandals you're wearing, Daisy, I wouldn't let my mother out in them."

Chapter Three

Bunty is a horrid little dog. I came into the kitchen this morning and she had climbed onto the dresser, ripped off the tinfoil and scoffed the bit of wedding cake Sandra brought over. Maybe the tinfoil will poison her.

Daisy was in tears because she and Johnboy rowed all night about the campervan holiday. Daisy is now convinced that going on holiday with Johnboy will shipwreck her reputation and get her excommunicated from our church. She thinks Reverend Robinson would refuse to marry them if he found out. Johnboy says she is frigid.

"He said we are always going backwards not forwards," she told us for the tenth time in succession. Mummy gave her two large fizzy tablets in a glass of water to calm her down. No one knew if they would do her any good so I took her into Magherafelt to buy a bottle of wine, a corkscrew, a box of chocolates and a packet of tampons.

Mummy said, "Daisy, you must realise that some people are more narrow minded than others. On our work outing to The Old Lammas Fair Bernie played the tin whistle and Siobhan played the banjo and we stopped in a pub on the way home. But of course they are Catholics."

Then she ate the most of Daisy's sweets and suggested that we do the Children's Church to take Daisy's mind off the row. She and Daddy were spending Sunday at Nutt's Corner Market choosing curtain material off the stalls for the new bungalow. Sarah was going to break the Sabbath and accompany them to ensure Mummy didn't buy everything brown and cream. Mummy has a thing about brown and cream. She says you can't see the dirt and it gives a room timeless elegance, and that everyone else has copied her and that's why the country is full of brown and cream sitting rooms.

"Hello boys and girls," said Daisy bravely, "who was born at Christmas?"

"Santa," said Colin Simpson, Willie's little afterthought brother.

"No," said our cousin Ernest, "it was baby Jesus and his brother God."

"Hi, Miss," said Colin, "Linda Jackson kissed the teeth out of me."

So I took Colin and some of the more disruptive elements to the back of the Sunday School where we played Hangman and talked about Heaven.

"My Aunty Eileen's sister lives in Heaven," said Colin. "Do you have sweets, Miss?"

"You aren't supposed to ask that question," said Linda Jackson, who had inherited most of Cousin Sandra's genes and absolutely none of Johnboy's. "In Heaven you sit around and look at the animals, Miss."

In the background I heard Daisy, "And Jesus said 'Bring those boys and girls to me...'"

"It was Unto Me," said Awful Ernest earnestly, "Jesus said 'Unto Me'."

"OK, Jesus said, 'Bring those boys and girls unto me,' and then he hugged and kissed them."

"The devil lives down below," Colin informed us

knowledgeably. "He has big horns. And I know what he does to you. He's got a big fire and he makes you shovel coal and your hands and clothes are black all the time. And there are no stairs."

"What is flying about in Heaven?" I persisted, to lighten the conversation.

"Birds," said Patience the minister's daughter, "and aeroplanes."

"Ghosts," said Colin who was beginning to wear me out.

"Fairies," said Linda Jackson.

"Ghosts, Miss, there are ghosts in Heaven," shouted Colin.

Fortunately for all of us, Willie himself stuck his head around the door and Colin stopped broadcasting mid-sentence and bolted. Children's Church was over for another week. There's a story that Willie took his mother to the hospital on the back of his motorbike when she was in labour with Colin. Willie was still wearing his "Proud to be a Protestant" vest, with his black leather jacket over it. The first time he wore a T-shirt to our church people fainted in the aisles.

"You know," said Daisy, "my hormones are killing Johnboy."

She phoned him and asked him to come over after dinner.

"This is not a 'Make Up Visit'," Johnboy informed her toughly when he arrived. "This is Make Up Your Mind Time. Either you come campervanning, or Willie and Helen and I are going without you. And that's final."

"You mean you don't care about your reputation, Helen?"

"Heaven has swings and see-saws and paddling pools," I said, "I'm still going."

Daisy deliberated with her conscience as she made Johnboy tea and I put on the video he'd brought with him.

"Do you have any hidden talents?" Johnboy asked me idly.

"I'm getting old," I said, "growing up. It's horrible. I bought clothes in Wallis yesterday. And I read one of Sarah's *Cosmopolitans.*"

"What is the furthest you have ever travelled?"

"I'll go," said Daisy suddenly, "please take me with you, Johnboy. And maybe we will find a crock of leprechaun gold at the end of an Irish rainbow."

"You are a crazy bitch, Daisy," Johnboy said, "and though it's bad when you go all conscientious on me it's worse when you come crawling back."

"You know," I interrupted prudishly, "I do prefer a film with no sex scenes."

Johnboy wasn't at all put out. "I'm trying to put Daisy in the mood," he explained.

Was it the film, or Daisy's tea, or Daisy's cigarette, or Daisy's conscience? I felt rather queer, dashed untidily upstairs to the bathroom. Was so green I frightened myself. Couldn't vomit. Always wondered why there was a chair in our bathroom. It's to sit on while you're throwing up. All that came up was water.

"Helen, what's the matter with you?"

The bathroom was cold. I spent the rest of the evening in bed wearing thermal pyjamas, the yellow velvet dressing gown, a wool cardigan over my shoulders, odd socks on my feet. And a duvet and a patchwork quilt and two blankets and a sleeping bag on top of me.

"It's no wonder you're sick, you stick," scolded Johnboy.

"People die of anorexia, Helen," Daisy reminded me.

"Well, there's no excuse for that," said Johnboy, "go and make her a feed, Daisy, and me one too."

"Keep your hands off my property," Daisy joked neurotically

when she came back with a feed and found Johnboy surreptitiously examining my ribs.

"But I like these provocative yet thermal pyjamas."

Now she was resolved to go, Daisy took her life savings to the bank to cash in as holiday money. For years she has been storing coppers in a plastic bag under her bed. The girl in the bank laughed when she saw the plastic bag but stopped laughing when she realised that she was going to have to count it. It took the whole morning because she had Irish money mixed in with the sterling and Sarah, who was driving, got tired waiting and told us we would have a horrible holiday because Willie Simpson eats like a pig and is disgusting. Sarah is only jealous because she is not invited.

When we got home Daisy returned the plastic bag to beneath the bed and asked me for the loan of a penny to start the collection all over again. Laura had left a note on the kitchen table.

Helen (11am), A hunky male voice phoned you, didn't leave his name. Aww! Sounded like an old friend? Said he might get in contact with you again.

Damn and blast. A man phones and doesn't leave his name, at eleven in the morning, and I'm not in the house. I felt really excited.

"Was he English?" I said, "or Irish, or Northern Irish?"

"He was a Belfastie," she said to my disappointment, "he was from the Department of Agriculture. It's about that job you applied for and didn't get. I just wrote that note for the laugh."

When Mummy and Daddy started building their brown and white bungalow everyone tried to get work to pay for it. The money I had made from *Chain Reaction*, My Novel That I Wrote, had dried up so I did an interview with the Ministry of Agriculture.

I have never been able to fully report on that interview. Certainly, Sarah drove me to Dundonald House and waited in the car while I walked into the room, took one look at that sad wall of grey faces, and panicked.

So the idiotic starter question, "Why have you applied for a post with the Department of Agriculture?" prompted the quick repartee, "The lure of the pension plan." rather than the much rehearsed "I feel I should use my degree". In desperate situations I often find refuge in being witty. And to the equally vague, "What strengths do you feel you could bring to the post of lecturer in Agricultural College?" I said, "Well, I learnt some karate when I was at university so there should be no problem."

How cringe-making to reflect on it. Why could they not have asked me cryptic things like, "If there were a hundred sheep in a field and one broke out, how many sheep would be left in the field?" Text book farmers don't know the answers to cryptic questions.

Of course it was their fault, the four faces on the panel. They encouraged me. The Chairperson was a literary buff, more fascinated by my opinions of the Booker Prize (and I said "Weren't the critics awfully bitchy about the books?") than my extensive knowledge of sheep. And hadn't I just spent the morning dipping ninety of the devils with Daisy? And the face burnt off me where the dip splashed up. No point telling them that. A prospective sheep lecturer should be following safety precautions to the letter, even to the extreme of "helmet with visor".

The panel told me that the advisory service was targeting the farm wife. I thought of Mummy; glamorous Mummy who still talked about ewes calving.

"You know," I told them in a burst of inspiration, "the farm wife has evolved somewhat from a fattie in a Crimplene dress who stands in the kitchen all day and cooks big feeds. She's glamorous now, and she has her own job and the only farming she sees is on *Emmerdale*. I don't think she would be much interested in doing her husband's Records and Accounts."

With hindsight I realise this was not the answer they were expecting. Nor was the family joke answer about my hobbies and interests. They all laughed nervously when I said I was a Captain in the Girls' Brigade and I stripped in my spare time.

I think I might have been a success at a dinner party but must grudgingly acknowledge that the Ministry are searching for high minded individuals who wear their 2.1 degrees on a banner across their neat grey-suited chests. My artistically flowery skirt and immaculately tousled hair may have impressed the man in them but not the interviewer.

I suppose I didn't really want the job.

After the interview Sarah and I walked for miles around Belfast looking for somewhere cheap to eat lunch. Eventually we ate in a pizza shop which was 50p cheaper than anywhere else. It still cost £11 each for a "creamy meat pasta" that was really mince and onions, and a ham pizza that Sarah swore was Spam.

"Tell him to take it away from me," she commanded.

I wondered why the Department had suddenly resumed interest. Perhaps one of the new lecturers had been attacked by the small fat boys and they could think of no one else fool enough to take the job.

"I don't know," said Daisy, "that time I did the PhD

interview, to be a Doctor of Organic Potatoes, the panel ground me so badly through the organic mill I had to be helped from the room afterwards. And then they offered me it. I would nearly be Doctor Gordon by now."

Then she realised the implications of me becoming employed.

"But Helen, if you get a job you won't be able to come campervanning and I will be unchaperoned with Johnboy. Why is life always so complicated?"

Chapter Four

"Helen," Mummy yelled from the bottom of the stairs, "there is a man on the phone for you."

The Ministry man I thought. He's going to pay me to educate adolescent boys.

But it wasn't the Ministry man. It was Brian from BMA.

Who?

Brian from BMA (Belfast Modelling Agency). Wanting to take me onto their books. To model clothes and food.

Me?

Brian wanted to know if I had a boyfriend or if I was married. A lot of the work would mean weekends away. Brian would be in Magherafelt this evening. He could call out to Derryrose and I could fill in the forms.

My hair dye had hardened to my head when Brian hung up. I hoped Brian liked his models with red hair.

"Daisy," I said, "I'm going to be a model." She was in her socks in the kitchen, a trail of straw followed her from her wellies at the back door, to the fridge, to the sofa.

She didn't hear me. "I'm having campervan breakdown," she said. "Last night I held a torch while Johnboy and Willie spent three hours fixing the heater. Then because it was dark we all sat in the van with the lights turned on just to see what it was like."

"What was it like?"

"Like a campervan with the lights turned on."

"Daisy," I repeated, snatching at her tub of chocolate chip ice-cream to get her attention, "I'm going to be a model."

"Milking aprons and wellingtons and stuff like that?"

"Don't be stupid. It wasn't the Department of Agriculture man. It was BMA. They are taking me onto their books. The man, Brian, is coming tonight to sign me up. I'm going to model clothes and food."

"He will be wanting the both of us then," said Daisy gloomily. "We could model the Slimfast Diet. Before and after."

What does one wear to receive a modelling agent? Casual, we all thought. Only if he wanted me to model a dog's dinner would I dress like one. Jeans and a shirt. Sarah was prised protesting from her Calvin Klein jeans, salvaged from Laura's American adventure. She advised the pink denim shirt with a white T-shirt beneath, not the blue denim shirt with the blue T-shirt beneath even though the blue T-shirt was Next.

The carefully tousled hairdo took ages to tousle and I couldn't pull a jumper over my head or sit outdoors in case it fell down again. And I couldn't eat in case I looked flatulent in the jeans.

The Department of Ag. man phoned during the preparations but I was rather vague with him. Who would choose to teach Harnessing The Ram when they could be in Barbados modelling sunshine?

"Daisy," I said importantly, "we will have to go on holiday soon. Before my career takes off."

I didn't read in case my specs left red marks. And I locked Bunty in my bedroom in case she jumped up on Brian when he came and scared him off before I got the contract signed.

But Brian never came.

Next day was a bummer and I lay naked on the roof reading *Where Angels Fear To Tread* and listening for Brian in case he came today instead. "Daisy," I informed her, when she came up to warn me that The Rabbit had arrived, "falling in love is a mere physical triviality, like warm sun or cool water."

"Helen," she quoted severely, "Johnboy and I are the 'likeness of what is perhaps eternal'."

Sandra was in an awful state. She had been run off her feet dusting the Royal Doulton and watching the gravel for a weed to sprout when the television licence inspector called. Panicking because she wasn't immaculately dressed she had slammed the door in his face and phoned her mammy for sympathy.

An hour later she got a phone call stating that the licence inspector had sustained a broken toe on impact with the solid oak front door and was now in hospital and was going to sue her. She had been asked to phone Mr C Lyons at a Belfast number once she got in contact with her solicitor.

"Sandra," I said, having given her a bottle of the mineral water she was so fond of, and phoned for her, "Mr C Lyons lives in Belfast Zoo."

Rain was jumping four inches off the road and thunder roaring overhead the day we left on holiday. I was ironing my Miss Selfridge via Oxfam dress, in case we visited somewhere exciting where I could wear it and show off my sunburn. Daisy, in more tears because of the weather, was packing her most unattractive clothes, so Johnboy would realise that she was a nice girl and didn't go off campervanning in sin with just anybody. Sarah had phoned sick into school so she could supervise the packing and make sure I didn't escape with any of her clothes.

There was a crack of thunder so loud that it blew the back door open and Bunty and Willie and Johnboy like the Apocalypse rushed in and trampled King Billie, my sleeping bag, borrowed from Uncle Reggie. Bunty, blood pouring from the side of her mouth, launched herself off the arm of the sofa and on to the ironing board to lick my mouth.

"I got her with the door of Roger," said Willie grabbing Sarah and turning her upside down, "I tried to run her down, but she was too cute." He flung Sarah onto the sofa and ignoring her protests flung himself down on top of her, dealer boots and all. Willie thinks that if he doesn't grope Sarah her ovaries will dry up.

"We are going to visit the Magic Hill first," said Johnboy plonking himself down at the table to eat the remains of the Ten O'Clock Tea tart, "in Gortin. But we will have to hold hands or the magic won't work. Go and make me some custard for this apple tart, Daisy."

They simultaneously leapt to attention when Mummy floated in. Men are instinctively gentlemen in Mummy's presence. Willie bounced up to give her a seat and Johnboy left the apple tart long enough to fling Bunty out of the back door.

Mummy ignored her daughters. She has been sulking in bed since Sunday, since Sarah wouldn't let her buy dark brown velour to make curtains for the halldoor in the new bungalow. Sarah insisted she buy a washed out, striped muslin, which she then draped artistically round a curtain pole. Mummy said she wouldn't have minded the muslin drapes so much if they had been any colours but green, white and gold. Daddy said that one comment, even in jest, from anybody, and the curtains were coming down.

So while Daisy packed the campervan and I pretended to

help her the Gruesome Twosome paid her exclusive attention and she thawed sufficiently to kiss us on leaving.

"Have a dolly holiday," she shouted as Roger ploughed out of the street.

It is a fact that once you begin to travel by campervan there seems to be a camper on every corner. Laura once said that when she was pregnant every third woman she met on the street was pregnant too. Willie and Johnboy roared "CAMPER" on each sighting to ensure Daisy, safe in the back making tea, didn't feel left out. I think myself that Daisy should have been squashed in the front beside Johnboy, flirting, not abandoned in the back making tea.

Willie Simpson has an endless love affair with his digestive system. We drank Earl Grey tea romantically beneath an umbrella on the roadside and across the road was Willie, cavernous nostrils and all, wolfing down a chip butty and chatting up the chancy thing he had bought it off. Johnboy, torn between two lovers, was drinking tea and gazing longingly at the chip-van and the chancy thing.

"I'm a friendly sort of person," Willie explained as we drove off again Gortin-ward and he helped himself to the left-over marmalade teabread.

We suggested pâté and toast and cold white wine by the Gortin lakes but Philistine Simpson kept driving and bundled us into a formica café for chicken burgers and tea and bread and butter. Eternally friendly, he again chatted up another chancy thing and draped himself provocatively over the counter while we sat alone at our grubby table and played with our grubby food. This time Johnboy succumbed to his baser instincts and the lure of the chancy thing. I employed all the resources of my imagination but the burger was definitely burnt, so Willie ate it for me, burnt bits and all, when he tired of chatting up the chancy thing.

It was at the Border crossing that the Drug Squad hauled us in. Johnboy was rallying Roger on, no time to browse through Belleek Pottery, no casual stroll through Castle Caldwell, we were rallying on to the Shamrock Chinese.

"Routine Inspection, Sir," the Drug Man told Johnboy and Willie, like a halfwit tied in the back of the van, stuck his head out of Johnboy's window to ask if that meant we could sample some drugs.

"Hi sir," said Willie as the sniffer dog scrambled through Roger, dog hairs and muddy paws flying. "Hi sir. This country is full of drugs. There's boys trafficking all the time. Everybody knows who they are but they are driving Mercedes, not campervans." He was mad to be stripsearched. "Fruits of Paradise here," he said and prepared to drop his trousers in front of us: the Drug Squad, and Daisy and Johnboy and me. I suppose an innocent person in such circumstances is entitled to a bit of fun. "No need for that, sir," said the Drug Man nervously.

"We just picked him up along the road," I explained to the handsome Drug Man who was going through my handbag, "could you arrest him by any chance?"

"No way," said the Drug Man flicking through *Bonjour Tristesse*. I suppose Françoise Sagan is not a drug trafficker's holiday reading.

"Maybe that Chinese wasn't a good idea, Helen." Daisy and I were squatting behind a rock on the beach. We were in Rossnowlagh, and Roger had been abandoned on the side of the road. Willie and Johnboy were chatting up a blond man with a jet-ski, hoping to be offered a spin.

"Do you think Willie will peep when we change for bed?"

"He has eaten so much today he might pop," I suggested hopefully. "I shall never be able to roll over in bed my belly is so full."

"It's terribly sad," I added savagely, "that the Drug Squad didn't arrest him to help them with their enquiries. He seems to bring the idiot out in Johnboy."

"Willie is OK," Daisy told me loyally. Daisy is a patient being. "He's just overexcited. And he has promised to cook breakfast tomorrow morning."

It's not only a man's heart that is won through his stomach.

That night I could not sleep. Roger's mattress was more uncomfortable than the ground. But not even my tossing and grumbling could deafen Willie's snores from the hammock above me. Daisy didn't know whether to be disappointed or relieved when Johnboy bagged the other hammock. She was sleeping angelically beside me. It is disgusting the way Daisy can sleep on a washing line. I'm in the Princess and the Pea league myself.

So I stoically sneaked out of Roger and onto the beach. Midnight and moonlight and an arch of cold stars. I don't know whose line that is. I'm sure it's not mine.

Suddenly Willie, nimble as a cat in Y-fronts, joined me. Willie in Y-fronts was the creation of my worst nightmare (at that moment).

He sat silently, obviously building up to something big, then said, "Helen, you have the ugliest feet that I have ever seen. Can't you buy a cream somewhere to make your toes grow longer?"

I opened my mouth to tell him to Piss Off (politely as we still had a week together in the confines of Roger) but then decided such pleasantries were unnecessary.

Sympathetically he said, "I'll make you a cup of tea," and before I could refuse he had Roger in action and the kettle boiled and the tea poured.

But it was probably the poteen in the tea that helped me sleep.

CHAPTER FIVE

For the first-time-lucky novelist there is always the temptation to tell of a holiday in the style of a travel report. In my diary I wrote, "There is rather a good view of Rossnowlagh Strand from the Cocktail Bar in the Cliffhanger Hotel" and "Try the Rum and Butter chocolate but not the Tea For Two in the Beach Cafe" and "The Cocktail Bar does not sell cocktails."

If I wrote of Rossnowlagh in this manner I would forget that I felt like a big person, part of the big view when I first saw the Strand from the Cocktail Bar and remember only the small person finding fault with Willie's flapping trouser legs. And I would try to forget that Willie ordered us all cocktails anyway and tutored the barman in their preparation. Willie is impervious to contempt.

And I have already forgotten how on the steep chugging climb from beach to bar, Daisy lost her head and leapt from Roger. Daisy has a panic attack thing about driving up steep hills. In the old Morris at home she used to hold the back door open for a quick getaway. It is her secret disappointment that no car has ever failed.

The petty irritations of Day One hit the hard boil in Sligo. All my impressionable life I have had a romantic love affair with Yeats. As Willie might walk miles for a mushy pea fritter, I would arise and go to Innisfree. I wasn't going to be American about the thing of course. No poetry postcards and signed photographs for me. But the chance to stand by a window in Lissadell House and imagine that he had stood there the day they invited him up for tea.

"Well frankly," said Willie Simpson, "I always thought Yeats was a pansy."

He was crunching his way through his second bag of crisps as our guided tour climbed the stairs at Lissadell.

"What the hell," I squeaked, "would you know about Yeats? Your idea of poetry is *Living In Drumlister.*"

How dare Willie Simpson presume to pontificate on my darling? Willie Simpson, living in Drumlister in clabber to the knee.

"He was still a pansy." Willie stuffed the crisp packet behind a case of stuffed birds and retrieved a Mars Bar from the pocket of his plastic coat. He wouldn't take the plastic coat off because it was new and he was afraid of someone stealing it.

"Did you know," he added, "that Yeats used to belong to a club where they weren't allowed to shift girls? No wonder he didn't catch Maud."

"Maud just didn't love him."

"I know that. Lots of men are in love with women who don't want them. I had the hots for Big Laura when we were seventeen but she wouldn't go out with me because I didn't have a car. William Butler should have stayed cool and played with his stiff upper lip. I bet Maud would have come running. There's nothing a woman likes more than a challenge. If he hadn't made it as a poet he would have been a hairdresser."

"How unfortunate for WB that he didn't have friends like you to advise him, Willie."

I loathe Willie Simpson. Even though he drove around for an

hour looking for Yeats's Grave for me. We eventually had to ask a couple of tinkers camping at the side of the road. They had never heard of Yeats but wanted to know if we would buy a lucky charm instead.

Finally we found it. I loathe Willie so much I will not join him in the Yeats Coffee Shop where he will demand bread and butter with his tea. Willie says only yuppies drink coffee.

I sat by His graveside and wept.

"Hi lady, lady." The two big tinkers from earlier, female perhaps but certainly not women, were approaching me at a speed not dissimilar to that of a buffalo stampede.

Help, I thought, I think that I shall meet my fate somewhere beside my idol's grave.

They clawed at my arm. The lucky charms were forgotten. Something about a starving baby and me having the face of a saint.

"I'm sorry," I was pathetically frightened, clinging to sunglasses and bum bag and peaked cap. "I'm not a tourist. I have no money."

Where was Willie now when I needed him?

"Willie! Willie!" I shrieked hysterically.

Wonderful Willie. Willie Rambo Simpson. He bolted from the Coffee Shop, threw away the last of his lolly, dashed to save me. God, he was magnificent. I clung to Yeats's headstone, spellbound while he Kung Fu kicked the buffaloes. Then he swept me into his arms and carried me half fainting back to Roger. I have never felt so romantic in my life.

Johnboy revved and revved at Roger and, as we took off in a skid of gravel, Willie poured his precious plum poteen down my throat as a lifesaver.

But once I was revived enough to tell him he was poisoning

me, he stopped being magnificent and started being Willie again. He even scolded me for handing the buffaloes my purse. He had had to pull a handful of hair out of one of them before she would give it back again.

"It's against my principles to hit women," he whined, "and I've never run away from a fight in my life."

He was quite upset.

Destination Salthill.

But it was a strangely subdued party who headed to Salthill. No *I Spy With My Little Eye*, no Atlantic 252, no idiotic discussions on our favourite packets of biscuits.

Miserably dizzy from poteen, huddled on the top of Roger's engine, light-headed from delayed fright, I couldn't tear my eyes from Willie's hands, the hands that had ripped the hair from that tinker's head. They reared magnificently from the cuffs of his plastic coat. The sort of hands a man could be proud of. Hands maketh man.

"Let's stop," Daisy said once, "let's stop and pull some blackberries," but no one answered her and no one acted like they had heard her. I was mesmerised by Willie's hands. Johnboy's, I noticed when we pulled in later, were bigger but they were too hairy to be magnificent.

Programmed to cook big feeds on cue, Daisy automatically began to make tea when Roger stopped.

"Stop it," I told her fiercely, "stop making tea like it was your job." But Daisy can be incredibly and stupidly stubborn sometimes. Treat them mean and keep them keen. It is her own fault if Johnboy ignores her. He has not tried to grope her in two days.

Salthill is the Portrush of Galway. I wore my Miss Selfridge via Oxfam dress. I was in a dangerous mood. Daisy was revving up to make more tea.

"Daisy and I are going out," I said, prising the kettle from her fist. "We've got dates with a couple of college boys. We're meeting them in town. Bye now."

"What did you say that for, Helen?" she protested bitterly as I frog-marched her out of the campsite. "We don't know anyone from Galway."

"Salthill is the Portrush of Galway, Daisy. There's men everywhere. And anyway did you not notice the Bridal Salon up the street? I thought we could call in on the way past."

Sarah says compromise is the work of the devil.

"But I'm not wearing a ring, Helen." Daisy paused modestly at the door, her nerve failing.

I felt tough. "We'll tell them you are having it cleaned."

Once inside, we were trapped.

"And what exactly do you have in mind, dear?" The wedding dress woman had made personal attention an art form, so I entrusted Daisy to her and entertained myself by pulling faces in the wall-to-wall mirrors.

"The bride always says, 'I feel comfortable in this one' before she chooses it," the wedding dress woman confided as Daisy pranced about in a flimsy chiffon and tulle creation with a huge hat and a hydrangea bush as a bouquet.

"Maybe I'd rather have something that makes me look like a bride?" Daisy suggested when she noticed my horrified face-pulling, "you know, with a veil and a train and a conventional white colour?"

The wedding dress woman says that white has lost popularity in the colour stakes because it "drains you". And I always thought it was because there were so few virgins left.

"Do you think Johnboy would like me in this?" Sixteen dresses later Daisy had discovered something that made her feel like a bride.

"Sure if he doesn't fancy you in it he doesn't have to marry you," I teased callously, "it's never too late to back out."

"But I can't wear something that Johnboy doesn't like," she protested as I dragged her screaming from the shop.

"Well, wait till he proposes and then worry about it." I had seen enough wedding dresses to convince me that Mummy's was satisfactory, empire line and orange stain on the cleavage and all. "Now let's go and find a couple of men somewhere."

"But we have a couple of men."

"A man is not a real man if his favourite hobby is looking up dirty words in the dictionary, Daisy." I bought us two strong drinks and reflected that I sounded a bit like Sarah saying that.

Whoring and touring. Incredible liberation after Willie's hands and Johnboy's thirst for tea.

A date with Daisy is always a festival of food, with me a feed of drink. A Travel Writer will tell you Salthill caters impressively for both tastes. My mother thinks it unnatural that young ladies might prefer each other's company to that of men. (Any men. Mummy is not particular provided they are male.) But then Mummy never had Willie and Johnboy as alternatives. I had to avoid Willie. I was beginning to fantasise about the arms attached to those magnificent hands.

"That Brian," said Daisy through a mouthful of lamb kebab, "the modelling agent that never came. Do you think he was an obscene caller?"

I nodded over the rim of my Budweiser bottle. She ate and I drank. "Or somebody pulling my leg. Like Willie Simpson."

I had to tell her. "Daisy," I said very casually, "did you ever notice Willie's hands?"

"No, what's wrong with them?"

I left it at that.

Daisy and I had eaten four different types of junk food between us and drunk in four different forms of hostelry (outside a pub, inside a pub, outside a hotel, inside a hotel) and we both were feeling rather full from food (her) and drink (me), when Willie's hands suddenly appeared over mine.

What a pleasing hallucination, I thought, right down to the blue plastic cuffs around the wrists. Turned around to tell Daisy who might appreciate the mysticism of such a moment. But she was fully occupied with a life-size Johnboy hallucination, and it was snogging her masterfully. The image of Johnboy, but without his sleazy and sexy moustache. And the hands were Willie's but he had got his hair cut. Willie didn't try to snog me.

"You women are impossible," announced Willie to the world. "Johnboy got his moustache shaved off because he thought Daisy didn't fancy him with it. You will get yourself arrested in that dress, Helen."

"Go away," I told him crossly, snatching my hands away from his. Bloody Daisy was still lost beneath Johnboy.

"I will arise and go now," said Willie impressively, producing a paper bag from his plastic coat, "but you had better come with me."

He threw me the bag. "Making-up present. The hairdresser gave it to me. We didn't take coffee in the barber's in case they charged us – so he gave us this perfume instead."

It was a freebie sample of Innisfree aftershave. "You can imagine you're Yeats when you wear it."

CHAPTER SIX

I consider myself a structured person. I need the security of saying, "We'll be in Dingle by Wednesday." Organisation, especially when I'm not the organiser, stabilises me. Spontaneity is horrible.

The Spontaneity camp, the "let's eat in Slatterys, demand a table in the porch, order drinks, discover it's a set menu, £35 a head, creep out with tail between the legs" group think my behaviour bizarre. They claim only Philistines are regimental, artists like me should have a freer spirit.

Quoting Mummy I informed them that anybody can write a novel, the country is full of first time novelists, I hadn't made enough cash to afford to be a free spirit.

We were in Tralee, drinking campervan tea and making plans. No, I exaggerate. We were in Tralee, drinking campervan tea and I was making plans.

"Willie," I said, "I know we planned to visit Dingle, but the shopping in Galway wasn't part of the plans and that took half a day."

In Moon's Daisy and I had rifled through a bargain bin of ladies' lingerie while Willie tried on women's sunglasses and Johnboy drenched himself with Poison.

"And," I added, "we spent far too long in those caves in Clare. And we told Jennifer that we would be in Kinelvin tonight."

"You mean," said Willie, "that you don't want to go to Dingle? When we planned to go there?"

Willie can be terribly tedious with his teasing.

"There's loads of seafood in Dingle, Helen."

It was my personal grievance that we had almost travelled the length of Ireland, and the closest I had got to seafood was fish and chips in Ennistymon.

"Oh really," I puffed, feeling like a cross old trout, "why can't we stick to the schedule?"

But the schedule fixed itself. I phoned Kinelvin to report on "Mutiny On The Roger"; to explain that my tenuous authority had been overpowered, the itinerary was abandoned, that we were making for Dingle, don't spare the horses.

Charlie, my sister's husband, said, "I've had the most marvellous idea, Helen." He sounded inspired, spontaneous even.

Oh no, I thought, not another one.

"Do tell," I said in a reserved, tight little voice, designed to dampen impulsive urges.

"Why don't Jennifer and I join you? Why don't the six of us go to Dingle together?"

Now, I like Charlie, and Daisy I suppose loves Charlie, but nobody, not even a sister who was a saint, would spend the night in a campervan with Jennifer. Jennifer is something else.

"Jennifer and Charlie are coming to Dingle with us," I told the rebellion, "is that spontaneous enough for you?"

Only Daisy's face didn't fall, but then Daisy's blood is thicker than water.

When Jennifer got into the campervan she wore a face Daisy and I recognised. It was her exploding face.

"Hello everybody, hello Daisy," said Charlie. Charlie has

beautiful manners. He contrasts delightfully with his wife. Jennifer didn't speak.

The road to Dingle, a quiet road, was paved with high emotion. Willie, showing off in front of strangers, had Roger bucking over hills and diving round corners. I was so scared I smoked a cigarette. Charlie talked farming and charmed Johnboy, and talked engines and charmed Willie. Apparently the Montgomery family used to drive a Hillman Hunter. Charlie once was arrogant and masterful, but then he married Jennifer. Jennifer smoked alone and didn't offer anybody her cigarettes. Sometimes I'm ashamed that she's my sister.

We all liked Dingle when we saw it. Even Jennifer smiled. I was so pleased to get there alive I noticed. Jennifer, I thought, was not at her best. And it was more than sulks. Jennifer looks magnificent when she's angry. But today she was pale and drawn.

Maybe, I thought with illuminating perception, maybe she is unhappy. Maybe she is regretting her hasty face-saving wedding, and gossip-thwarting flight to Kerry. They hadn't even had a honeymoon. She was too young to be a mother. She was lonely in Kinelvin, surrounded by men, always having to fight to keep standing.

"Jennifer," I said, "would you like a beer?"

"Yes."

Mummy had tried to beat "please" and "thank you" into her.

Jennifer's and Charlie's eyes met briefly. He was frowning like he didn't want her to drink but didn't dare tell her to stop.

But Jennifer wasn't a drinker. She was the only Gordon, Sarah included, who often left a glass unfinished. She considered drink a social necessity which weakened her willpower and resulted unfavourably in babies.

"There's definitely something the matter," I told Daisy in the ladies' loo, "something important, not just temper."

"I know," she sighed. "She is making Charlie awfully miserable. He keeps such a brave face on it too."

"Daisy, why are you taking his side? Why do you always make excuses for Charlie? He used to make your life a misery."

"But he's buying us dinner tonight," said Daisy.

Jennifer's face didn't lighten during dinner. She picked at her sorbet assortment and wouldn't join in the photograph of us grouped around the lobster tank. And just after the food arrived, and Willie was making castration jokes and brandishing his pliers, she bolted from the table and the revelry around her.

"Jennifer seems a bit off colour," I said to Charlie.

"She's fine," said Charlie carefully.

Jennifer was not fine. She was the colour of mud when she returned to the table.

"I'm fine," she snapped at me, "I drank too much last night."

I knew I was being boring, but it was too easy to believe her.

"You know what irritates me most about these pretentious new rich restaurants that are springing up everywhere?" Charlie changed the subject smoothly, "I mean when I'm in a good mood it actually amuses me that there is never vinegar on the table."

"I don't think it's politically correct to eat your chips with vinegar anymore," I suggested.

"And don't you notice that roast potatoes are now fashionable?" Willie added, forking a couple of mine to accompany his lobster, "Helen's plate here is overflowing with them."

"But it's delicious," Daisy interrupted expansively, "all of it." If you are buying Daisy food she will think a burnt chicken burger tastes good.

"Are you planning to go through Dublin on the way back?" Charlie's conversational capacity impressed me enormously. "I was in town last week. Saw *Great Expectations* at the Strand. My favourite love story. Arty farty stuff you know, but after forty winks at the start I saw nearly all of it."

"We did *Great Expectations* for my English O Level," Johnboy informed us intelligently. "We saw a film of it too, but I was so busy courting Lorraine Scott at the back of the school hall I failed."

Roger sleeps six on two double beds and two hammocks. Since their reunion in Salthill Daisy and Johnboy have been learning to sleep together. They plant their sleeping bags side by side, so there is the possibility (though less probability) of touching in the night. Jennifer and Charlie have a double bed licence. This left Willie and I to chill out in the hammocks.

But before we got into bed Jennifer erupted. Charlie said, "Let me give you a leg up into the bed, darling," and she went completely berserk. I was petrified, like with the tinkers only worse because Jennifer had a civilised, church-going upbringing, same as me. It wasn't a lover's quarrel either because Charlie wasn't fighting back. He was just holding her off him and talking to her quietly. The time Daisy and I visited Kinelvin Jennifer's filly kicked Charlie so hard she knocked him over, but he didn't even raise his voice. Gypsy, Daisy's mare, kicked me once when I was trying to catch her on fresh grass. I kicked her back and bruised my toes through my wellie boot.

There's something about a married couple fighting that I find obscene. It's not the same with boyfriends. Laura and Mick of the Shovel-Like Hands used to tear strips off each other when they were drunk and that never annoyed me. It's because they are married, I think they should respect each other more.

I feel no sympathy for unprovoked violence. Her explosion

disgusted me. I wanted to slap her though I couldn't imagine it doing much good.

Charlie was so impassive.

"Love knows no limit to its endurance, no end to its trust. No fading of its hope. It can outlast anything." But Charlie wasn't religious.

"Charlie has another woman."

Jennifer had insisted that we take a walk before breakfast along the beach. I really thought she was going to tell me she was pregnant again. Jennifer is such a fertile female. All night when I couldn't sleep I had thought of suitable answers for "I'm pregnant again".

I couldn't understand "Charlie has another woman". I said nothing. She didn't expect me to.

"Why do you think he was in Dublin last week watching love stories? He acts as if nothing is different, Helen. He says he wants to go away with her for a few days. To satisfy his curiosity."

"What's he curious about?" What a bizarre situation.

Jennifer laughed suddenly. "I knew I could depend on you, Helen, to be trivial about the whole thing. I don't know a damn what he's curious about."

Would it be very callous to ask who the woman was? Probably one of the hunting crowd, a glamorous hunter, not a horsy one. It's easier to understand obsession for a beautiful person. And Jennifer says it's all fights and fornication round horses.

"You'll never guess who it is."

"You mean I know her?"

"Oh yes, we all know her. Maybe if Charlie had got into her bed instead of into mine when we were at UCD I'd never have had to marry him."

Elisabeth?

"Elisabeth," said Jennifer. "I know she's your friend but she really is a dirty tart, Helen. She doesn't even fancy Charlie. She's just sampling forbidden pleasures. And he's that stupid he can't see through her. It's really pathetic."

Elisabeth Churchill-Knox, Figure of Romance, my friend. Elisabeth is very golden and very suitable. Richard Knight is engaged to a friend of ours, Elisabeth Churchill-Knox – "You'll never believe this, I'm marrying Richard."

The dirty tart. I said, "It must be confusing for her. Richard and Charlie and whoever else is following. Does she play them off against each other?"

An affair is only fun when you aren't involved in it. I was involved. It was only puppy love or something with Richard but I was still involved. Dirty. Dirty.

Charlie didn't falter when Jennifer, with tantalising aloofness, declared that she was running away with the campervan.

"As opposed to the circus?" he smiled.

If she hadn't been my sister and therefore incapable of telling lies I would have said he was like an innocent flower, not a serpent under it.

I didn't want Charlie to be a bastard. It shattered his stereotype. But, to quote Daisy, who was still unaware of her idol's fall from grace, blood is thicker than water, so Jennifer had to be right.

"What about Freddie?" asked Daisy.

"My husband can mind his son."

And with that the subject closed.

Chapter Seven

"You were quite right to leave him. He'll soon come crawling back."

Mummy and Daddy were rowing, something to do with the windows for the brown and white bungalow, I think. Or that was how it started. Daddy threw a wobbly when he discovered they were double-glazed, Daddy wanted to hear the birdies singing when he was lying in bed, he said. Very environmental my father. The day we got home in Roger it was hailstoning and he had met us at the door with "Every hailstone kills a little flower." Sometimes we wonder about him.

Jennifer, my strange proud sister, had insisted we tell no one of Charlie's infidelity. It was to be our little secret, she said. To everyone, even Mummy, Jennifer was still a hard-faced, hard-hearted, hard-headed harlot. Carved from stone and eternally selfish.

Jennifer said, "I've left him behind. I've come home. I never want to see him again."

"Men are a botheration," Mummy confessed as one wife to another. "You can't live with them and you can't live without them."

Laura, our magnificent example of a woman who could indeed live without her husband, spoke up. "Now Mummy, Even though you're not speaking to him, you needed Daddy's dental surgery yesterday. He solved the Mystery of the Frozen Mouth for you."

Apparently Mummy had been back at the dentist getting her false tooth checked and he sneaked a couple of quick fillings in when he got her trapped in the tipping chair. Four hours later her mouth hadn't defrosted and she was so worried she wrote Daddy a little note asking him to examine her mouth for her. In silence he sterilised his hands with boiling water and examined her mouth only to find one of the cotton wool swabs was still in it.

"In fact," said Laura proudly, "I am the only person I know who has successfully deserted her husband. I have never taken up with another man."

Isn't life cruel the way it lets you make sweeping statements? And then they get thrown straight back in your face.

It was a front page story in both local papers on Thursday. "Lady In White Walks – Ghost seen on Heather Hill".

"I suppose she is a lonely soul in immortality," said Laura at lunchtime. She had bought both newspapers, the Catholic and the Protestant. Ghost-sighting is a cross-community effort. "I bet she's some girl who has deserted her husband and can't get into Heaven without him. And she's walking Heather Hill trying to remember where the pub is so she can bring him home. It says here that several reputable people have seen her. I suppose that means they were sober."

"The poor creature," said Mummy, who was as excited as Laura about the sighting, but too mean to buy both papers. "Has anybody tried to help her yet?"

"Of course not. Reputable people don't have the stomach for the supernatural."

I knew what was coming next. They were thinking the same thing.

"Let's go tonight."

"No way," I said firmly, "I'm a reputable person. I would die with fright."

"But Helen, you are the only one of us who will see her. Mummy and I never see ghosts. We are too cynical."

"I know. That's why I'm not going with you. Daisy sees them sometimes. Take her instead."

"That's no good. Daisy never sees them unless she's with you."

"Come on, Helen. It'll be a bit of crack."

I used to think a lot about ghosts. I read a book once, at an impressionable age, about a woman, Louise, whose son Edward died and she locked herself away and wept until she almost touched him. She could see him and talk to him but just missed touching him. For weeks afterwards I dreamed the ghost of the dead boy was coming in through the bedroom window. I was too frightened to get out of bed, too frightened to lie in the dark, I could only sleep when I had a Bible in bed with me.

Still, I knew Mummy and Laura wouldn't give me a minute's peace until I agreed to go ghost hunting with them. I think I see them because I used to sleepwalk as a child.

"OK," I said, "OK, I'll go."

Thursday was a good ghost-sighting night. With dirty weather all day it started to get dark about five o'clock. Phantom mists hung from Daisy's clothes when she came in from the milking, and gnawing panic squeezed my gut every time Laura mentioned The Lady In White.

"Maybe you should get out of the car, Helen – so she can see you."

We were parked on Heather Hill. The papers had said that

she always appeared between eleven and midnight but we had been there since ten in case she came early and I was foundering in the back of the Escort. Stupid of me not to bring a hot-water bottle. Mummy wouldn't let me bring Bunty because she says ghosts are frightened off by dogs barking.

"Yes, Helen, you get out and call her."

"But what if she creeps up on me from behind?" I protested, "and taps me on the shoulder with ghostly fingers? What if you panic, Laura, and drive off and leave me with her? She might bewitch me or something."

"I won't be scared if I see her," Laura boasted. "Isn't that why I'm driving? Because I'm rock solid steady. You jump when you see mice, Helen. And Mummy, no offence, but you can't be trusted to keep your head either. To be honest I'd be more scared of another car running into the back of us in this mist."

"Oh stop squabbling, girls," Mummy interrupted. She was staring fixedly out of the window, through the mist which was creeping round the car. "We might miss her, or scare her off with all the noise."

And then I saw It. In front of the car. A figure in white coming straight at us.

"Get out, Helen," Mummy yelled, "she's stopped. She's going to run away if you don't get out. Get out and talk to her."

All those years of discipline. "Do as I say, not as I do."

All those spankings. "Delayed obedience is disobedience."

All that church. "Honour your father and your mother."

"No way," I said, "get out yourself."

Laura, assuming command, wrenched the Escort into gear, flattened her foot to the floor and drove straight at The Lady.

"Ghostie! Ghostie!" she yahoo-ed, "we're coming to get you."

There was an almighty bump, a very human scream (I think

it was mine) and The Lady in White flew straight over the roof of the car.

"Oh dear," said Laura, "hold tight," as she handbraked the Escort round.

We all leapt out. I wasn't a bit scared. If the car had gone straight through the ghost I would probably have been bad with my nerves for the rest of my life.

It was Willie Simpson.

"Willie Simpson," said Laura in her Special Voice. At fifteen she had used it with Reverend Robinson. At twenty-two she had used it with The Yank.

She hadn't fallen in love again, had she? With Willie Simpson, Willie of the marvellous hands and the cavernous nostrils?

"Willie Simpson, you great big beautiful man," and she kissed him.

Now I'm not making excuses for her but Laura's nature deserves explanation. Since adolescence she's had a fiendish desire to shock people, and aristocratic disdain for what they think of her. So far so good. Mummy has kept young inventing plausible excuses for her wilful behaviour. You must understand that in Derryrose people do not act on impulse, are never carried away by lustful passions, and never walk away when things don't turn out right.

It's for better, for worse; for richer, for poorer, till death do us part in Derryrose.

To cut a long story short she moved in with Willie Simpson. To live with him. In sin. I'm not making excuses for her. We Gordons neither condoned nor condemned her. If Mummy tiptoed on the edge of a breakdown and Daddy existed in a permanent state of "wobbly" no one guessed outside the door of Derryrose. They presented a very royal front to the scandal I thought; cowering in the house convinced the country was talking about them and marching us all straight to the front of the church every Sunday so "they" could appreciate our solidarity.

"I don't like him a bit," said Laura, "but he fascinates me. Imagine dressing up like The Lady In White and pretending to be a ghost the very night you and I go ghost-hunting. It was predestination."

"And I suppose your wanton behaviour was predestined too?"

"Of course it was. Predestination, and the size of his hands. Big hands are a real family weakness, aren't they Helen? Have you ever noticed the size of Willie's? They are even bigger than Mighty Mick's, who I shifted at university."

"Can't say I've noticed." I changed the subject. "Sandra Flemming brought the new BMW over yesterday to offer us her condolences."

"Was she practising her evangelising on you?"

"She told us that her wedding service was the most memorable and important part of her marriage. She is deeply saddened by your behaviour. Does nothing move you about the Christian Faith, Laura?"

"The self-righteous upstart," Laura was gobsmacked. "What did you say to her?"

"Listen to me. She and Ian are praying for us and will support us through everything, but she feels she would be compromising her witness in the community to associate with you anymore."

"And what did you do?"

"I didn't do anything. I was writing it all down to put it in a book some day. It was Sarah. She went into orbit. She said, 'How wonderful that you are so spiritually confident, Sandra, that you take the plank out of your eye and stone my sister with it. I suggest you go back to your big cold house and your big cold husband and pray for yourself'."

"She did not say that. You're making it up. Sarah never swears."

"She did. She was magnificent."

"I wish I was there. What did Sandra do?"

"As Sarah suggested I suppose." I was so relieved to unburden the incident on Laura. Laura needed to be warned. Derryrose was out to get her.

"Have you gone back ghost-hunting yet?" I asked.

"You know, Willie and I have been up and down Heather Hill every night since and there has been no Lady In White."

"What can you expect? The noise of Willie's motorbike is bound to be scaring her off. Mummy went ghost-hunting last night and she says you and Willie roared past her and Willie wasn't wearing a stitch of clothing. She swears you were dressed in a purple net curtain, like a Biker Chick from Hell. Where did Mummy learn words like Biker Chick from Hell?"

Laura giggled. "Mummy thinks she's a mature student because she's doing that Biology O Level. Remember when the Zimbabwe Rugby Team came to the Rainey and I shifted the big black one who was staying with Ian Flemming? Ian brought him to Sunday School the next day and Mummy kept saying that he had beautiful eyes, like a cow. And then she went to the match to check he was black all over. She wore her fur coat. I'll never forget it."

"She never used to take that fur coat off. You told me she was having an affair with Dr Hunt because she always wore it to the surgery. I wonder what animal it was."

"Well, whatever it was it could have walked to the Rainey itself, Mummy wore it there that often. Willie says even he remembers it."

"When we were campervanning Willie said he used to fancy you but you wouldn't go out with him because he didn't have a car."

"I wouldn't go out with him because he was a guttersnipe. And because his mother is Slack Alice Simpson. Now I realise a well-laid woman can forgive her man anything. Isn't it marvellous the way you can look at someone for years and never really see them?"

Chapter Eight

The Laura-gate scandal diverted wagging tongues. Hitherto they had been speculating about Jennifer's reappearance. Everyone knew Jennifer was married – hadn't Laura's waters broken as Jennifer said "I Do" – so where was the good-looking husband with the beautiful speaking voice?

How mundane their existence would be without us big girls at Derryrose to gossip about. And our mother not half-wise either.

"Do you think he has gone away with her?"

It had been the longest fortnight in living memory. Jennifer made sure we suffered, because she suffered. I tried to remain sympathetic because I knew the whole story; everyone else's patience had dried up.

"Jennifer," Mummy pleaded, "you've taught him a good enough lesson. Phone him and make up."

Mummy has no fire in her belly. She always stalls on the brink of no return, and gives in in the end.

"Don't be so wet, Mummy."

"But Jennifer, you are making my life a misery. You fight with your shadow. You never wash a dish after yourself. We've only just managed to get rid of Laura and now you've landed in on us."

Jennifer shrugged, "When Laura left The Yank you welcomed her home with open arms."

"If you care to remember, dear, we told everyone at the time that he had died. No one has ever guessed that she deserted him."

"Helen, do you think he has gone away with her?"

I have a guilty secret. Elisabeth has written to me from Paris. I got the letter the day before yesterday and I've been hiding it between the pages of *Anna Karenina*.

She says "we" were in London looking for a wedding dress but found nothing, so "we" went on to Paris. This mysterious "we" threads throughout the whole letter. It could be her mother of course, or it could be Richard, but it's probably Charlie. Elisabeth has a talent for telling you things without actually saying them. The bit at the end of the letter worries me the most.

"Darling Helen, my truest friend, will you be my bridesmaid? And Laura. And Daisy. Three pretty maids all in a row. You will be visually stunning surrounding Richard and me."

"Well, if he has gone away with her, Jennifer, he's bound to be back again by now. He'll be missing the hunting."

"I shouldn't think so. Charlie gets really green with nerves on hunting mornings. I usually have to spoonfeed him his porridge and tie his stock. I tried giving him an egg once but he vomited rings round him."

I screwed up my nose, "And they talk about the unspeakable chasing the inedible. No wonder Daisy is an Anti."

"Oh, Charlie is fine once he gets on his horse, and gives its mouth a good jerk. Apparently the first time he hunted he had a leaking appendix but his father made him ride anyway. Told him if he didn't get on his pony he would take a stick to the pony first and then to Charlie."

I felt faintly ill. Not because Charlie had been bullied on to his pony, the same was common practice at Derryrose. I had returned from a week with Aunt Maisie once to find a brand new whip waiting for me, and had cried with fear. But it was little wonder with such a dominated past that Charlie could be seduced by a temptress like Elisabeth.

"You know, when we were in Roger," I said, because I was bored talking about Charlie, "we ran over a fox, and Willie was going to skin it and fry it just to see if it was inedible. Daisy threw a real wobbly and attacked him with the wheel-jack so we had to bury it instead."

"I'm missing the hunting," Jennifer scowled, "far more than I'm missing Charlie. That fat pony of Daisy's has no brakes, no manners and no mouth."

"The Rabbit has a horse. You could ride it."

Sandra Jackson's meteoric ascent to the Flemming dynasty had included the acquisition of Moonlight. One can see and be seen so much better from the back of a well-groomed horse. Sandra, who takes private riding lessons in Fermanagh, is willing to trot Moonlight for short periods on tarmac but refuses to canter along the grassy verges at the side of the road. One time Moonlight bucked her off when Johnboy went roaring past in the tractor.

She rides a horse as if she learnt how to do it out of a book. Anything we learned was through falling off. Her childhood is not pimpled with nightmare pony scenarios, her father never stood in the middle of a forty-acre field yelling, "Hold the little beast, you boring child, he's making a fool of you," like ours had.

"Charlie's father wasn't really much worse than ours when

you think of it, Jennifer. Moonlight is a lovely animal, you know. Sandra can't ride him at all. Johnboy says she wanted an old half-dead thing from a trekking centre in the Mournes but Ian wouldn't buy it for her because it wasn't dear enough."

"Poor Scaredy-Cat Sandra," Jennifer rubbed her hands. "I bet she hasn't burnt rubber on him once for fear of falling off on her bony bum. I'll tell her it's my Christian duty to take him out. Life is no fun unless you live dangerously."

How I wished she would make up with Charlie and go back to Kerry. I wanted to discuss the bridesmaid thing with Laura and Daisy. We had all lived with Elisabeth in Dublin in college days. Jennifer had lived with her too but maybe Elisabeth thought that four pretty maids all in a row would be a plaster. We were going to look silly anyway. Laura and Daisy are a lot bigger and fatter than me. In a row with them I would look stunted, the runt of the litter. And what colour would she want us in? In her flamboyant youth Elisabeth wore tablecloths and curtains.

"Pre-Raphaelite," said Elisabeth.

Finally I had phoned her from the call-box on the Toomestone Road. Articulated lorries and school buses whizzed past as we talked. Jennifer had swallowed her pride, sucked up to Sandra and was, as we spoke, giving Moonlight the ride of his life.

"You know Pre-Raphaelite, Helen. Brocade and bright colours and elaborate tapestries."

"And long red hair and long white noses?"

"Stop reading the small print, Helen. When will you come to Dublin for a fitting?"

The strangest thing about Elisabeth's marriage plans is not her lack of fidelity, it's her lack of a date. She says she wants everything ready so that someday when the sun is shining they can go for it.

I don't know what her secret is with Richard, that he puts up with this nonsense. Richard belongs to my school of structured thought. Or he used to.

"So, how was Paris?" She was costing me a fortune, standing on this windswept noisy roadside chatting to her. But at least Mummy couldn't yell at me to hang up or pull the cord at a juicy bit, or try to strangle me with it as she did Jennifer the other day. Jennifer was on the phone for an hour to Sandra before she was offered a "ride out" on Moonlight. Sandra was so shocked by Sarah's outburst she and Ian don't think us suitable friends anymore.

"Paris is always Paris," said Elisabeth nonchalantly. Such familiarity made me wonder how often she "shopped" there.

I told Laura about Elisabeth and Charlie. Intimate secrets bore me eventually and one thing about Laura, she never suffers from blinkered vision.

"I'm sure she was in Paris with Charlie," I gossiped, "yet she has the audacity to write and invite us to her wedding. Her head is still in the clouds."

Laura shrugged. She was strangely subdued. "Elisabeth's cloud hasn't let her down yet. The rest of us are using parachutes."

"Has your rush of lust for Willie worn off already? People will say you are giddy, Laura."

"Don't you start, Helen. I'm only living in sin. You'd think I was the first to do it. Mummy boiled in here earlier when Willie and I were eating Sugar Puffs and watching the cartoon *Hamlet*. She was nicey nicey to him of course but once he went to work she wept for an hour. Bitch. She knows rightly if she shouts I'll laugh but I can't bear to watch her crying. She looks so ugly and snottery. Mummy says it's all her fault I've become an adulteress. She should never have educated me. If I'd never discovered my brain I would never have thought of running away with Willie. I hate it when she does the 'I'm only doing it for your good dear' talk."

"She's just embarrassed that it's Willie Simpson you are living with, Laura. We all are. He is still a yahoo even if you are living with him."

"Oh I know all that, and we live in a mobile home in Simpson's yard and all her self-righteous girlfriends don't speak to her anymore, or else they are praying for her and that's worse. There should be euthanasia for the lot of them. Especially Aunt Maisie. The old battle-axe swanned in here yesterday, leopard skin coat and all. She doesn't give a hoot that I'm sinning, but Willie is 'socially undesirable' according to her. I'll never understand why Mummy and Aunt Maisie hate each other. They are both upstarts. Willie has an O Level in Psychology and he writes poetry. Mummy watched the whole of *Hamlet* and then said, 'Was Ophelia *Hamlet*'s mother?'"

"Laura, is that all that's bothering you? Our mother and Aunt Maisie?"

"Hardly. Willie says we can't relax together, I want to play Doctors and Nurses with him and he wants to change the diff on his stockcar."

"They say the first year is the worst, Laura. Why don't you and Willie get a cheap ring in Argos with a fourteen day money-back guarantee and tell people you've got engaged? You could wear it round Magherafelt and to church and then take it back and get your money back. Miss Churchill-Knox wants us down to Dublin before Christmas to be fitted with red wigs and long noses. You could tell people you bought the ring down there."

Laura scowled. "I don't want to get engaged to keep my mother happy. She's threatening to have my twins taken away from me. And Johnboy's mummy won't let him play with Willie anymore. Maybe she won't let him out to play with Daisy either."

I tell you something. Child-wise, Laura's moving in with Willie Simpson was a gift from God. Scarlett and Shaun are abominable infants.

"I'm sure she's only bullying you about the twins. Daddy would throw a wobbly if she brought them back to Derryrose. Mummy's getting a very hard time from him. You know he won't say anything to your face. He slippy-tits to her and makes her do all the shouting. He's afraid he won't get on the church committee with you in such a compromising position."

"Oh, I know how to get round Daddy," Laura informed me comfortably – Laura was always Daddy's brown-eyed girl – "I'm going to join the band again."

After motorbikes and poetry, Derryrose Accordion Band was Willie's favourite toy. And Daddy, as Worshipful Master of Derryrose LOL 123, is so hugely dependent on its musicians to lead his Sons of Ulster that he spends Tuesday nights taxiing them to and from the practices Willie and Slack Alice organise. When he really wants to drive Mummy mad he plays the big drum at band parades, taking turns with his friend Johnny Paisley.

"Will you be drumming with Willie," I asked politely, "or playing the accordion alongside Slack Alice?"

"Actually I thought I would lead it. Far more glamorous than being lost in a bunch of accordions and I won't have to go to practices. I plan to wear your tennis skirt and those red high heeled boots Mummy bought herself but never had the nerve to wear."

"Linda Jackson always leads our band," I protested, "she even served her time carrying the strings of the banner. Auntie Eva will scratch your eyes out."

"Auntie Eva hasn't a hope. Linda Jackson is big enough to carry an accordion this year even if she's not smart enough to play it. And anyway I'm sleeping with the band master."

CHAPTER NINE

Jennifer grew a rash of pimples to complement the dark rings under her eyes. I couldn't escape from her, we slept together. Sometimes in the middle of the night she would moan "Charlie". I always got out of bed at this point in case she took a grab for me, and prayed frantically on my knees on the floorboards that Charlie would ride up and fetch her.

It was now less than a week till the dress fitting date in Dublin with Elisabeth.

"Disagreements and anger come from bodily lusts, Jennifer," I told her on Saturday afternoon, the day she threw Twinkle, Mummy's cat, head first out of an upstairs window. "Why don't you and Laura form a Runaway Wives Club and talk about How It Used To Be?"

I stomped out of the house to her screams of "I'm not making the first move!" and cut cross-country to the Toomestone telephone box to telephone Kinelvin. In my own little way I'm as much of a slippy-tit as Daddy but rather more independent in my planning.

"Bonjour Charlie," I said the minute he lifted the telephone, "comment Paris? If you love your wife as much as married couples are supposed to love each other then I suggest you come crawling back and get her."

I put the phone down. Pity I couldn't have been really anonymous and spoken entirely in French, but it was never on the French O Level syllabus – how to make threatening phone calls in a foreign language.

I joined Willie in the chip-shop where he was buying a curry chip for his loved one and burgers for himself. He treated me to a fish supper and offered me a lift home on the back of his motorbike. I'm a bit of a biker-chick myself.

Willie dropped me off and I crouched in the porch at the front door to eat my chips in peace. So when Charlie phoned I could hear himself and Jennifer's conversation clearly from the hall. What he said to her gave me a funny heartache feeling that I couldn't understand. He was still talking when I sneaked round the back of the house. It was obscene to listen in to such a conversation. As I came into the kitchen Jennifer was screaming something disgusting and Mummy, Daisy and Sarah were pressed to the hall door listening.

Mummy, who believes herself to have the wisdom of Solomon concerning human nature, mouthed, "Hell hath no fury like a woman scorned."

Jennifer crashed in through the door. "I knew you would all be bloody listening!" she screamed, "go to Hell the lot of you!" There was a lot of banging as she bolted outdoors towards Gypsy's stable. Sandra is threatening the Animal Welfare because Jennifer brought Moonlight back black with sweat and lame the only time she rode him. The exercise nearly killed both of them.

She returned about an hour later filthy dirty and soaking wet. "Have a loan of my hairdryer," I suggested as she slumped onto the bed, dirty boots and all. "Did you fall off?"

"Yes, into a puddle. God, Helen, he is the most inconsiderate creep I know, he's self-righteous and hypocritical..."

"And all those tears are your heart interrupting."

"He only phoned to check I had enough money."

"Who made the very first move?"

That night I didn't sleep for hours and she didn't sleep at all and we lay side by side and didn't tell each other. I felt very nervous and excited about something and my eyelids were too jumpy to shut them. Jennifer breathed very slowly to pretend she was sleeping. I don't know why she was ashamed of being upset. A man/woman relationship is the most wonderful thing in the whole world. I often feel I'm missing out not having one.

Next morning the effect was woeful. Two pairs of puffy red eyes arrived down to breakfast.

Jennifer smoked three cigarettes in a row, pulled Sarah's hair when she complained about passive smoking and lung cancer and went outside to ride Gypsy in defiance of Mummy's decree that we all continue to attend church.

"Don't let her get to you, Sarah," I said because I feel a bit sorry for Sarah sometimes. I am afflicted with family sympathy. They are all walking disasters. The only one I never feel sorry for is Great Aunt Maisie but it worries me that I might turn out to be like her.

Even Laura and Willie went to church that morning, and never was there a pair that looked less like penitent sinners. Laura, fashionably late, flounced to the front and squashed in beside Mrs Reverend Robinson and all the little Robinsons. I heard her whisper, "Rachel, I'm freezing. I'm going to have to wear trousers in future."

The reek of fag smoke and drink nearly knocked me out when she joined me at the church door afterwards.

"Do you think if Daddy stood beside His Reverence and pressed five pound notes into all those shaking hands that he would get on to the church committee?"

I suggested that she make an elegant exit before Reverend Robinson and the Rabbit Flemming organised a stoning party for her.

"Ah Helen, don't be so unchristian. We had great crack last night in Ballyronan. It was the District Orange Dinner Dance. They held it in the shed behind Grubb's pub. Aunt Maisie and Bobby Lennox were there too. Willie and I rocked the Port-a-loo when Aunt Maisie was using it. We thought we had killed her. She was so cross when she came out she threw a chair at me."

"Maybe you should go home, Laura," I repeated anxiously as Mummy and Eva Jackson came out of the church together, "Eva is probably trying to get Mummy to join that Women's Group again and you know how cross she makes her."

"What was Mrs Jackson on about?" I asked when we got into the Escort to go home, "She was so busy talking to you she didn't even shake hands with Reverend Robinson."

"That's because she is completely disgusted with him. She says she never heard a sermon like it in her life. I was rather impressed myself."

"The bit about circumcision was OK," said Sarah, "but I thought the other unsuitably vague. It's not politically correct to describe a menstruating woman as unclean."

"Well, I thought it was magnificent," Mummy argued, "especially the bit about women being forgivably irritable at certain times of the month. I nudged your father so he didn't miss it."

"Well, he was right about that bit," Sarah conceded. "Last month I sellotaped Colin Simpson's mouth for talking in class."

"What surprises me," I said, "is that Eva didn't like it. I thought that was the sort of militant chat Women's Groups always go over."

"If only," said Mummy, "I might be tempted to join. But Eva's group press flowers and write poetry and this week they are going to learn how to stuff and de-bone a chicken."

"That sounds like quite good fun," Daisy and I said together.

"Of course," said Mummy, "it's my fault you are such creative children. I used to sit with you when you cut things out of magazines and drew pictures and wrote stories. Even Laura is good at knitting. Only Jennifer was never creative but she was far braver than any of you. She learnt to ride a bicycle the first time she got on it."

Back at the ranch the potatoes were still sitting raw in the scullery sink and Twinkle was sleeping in the saucepan.

"The tinker," Mummy screamed. She was suffering an irritable phase that day. "If I catch her I'll kill her with my bare hands." She wrenched open the kitchen door and advanced into a suffocating haze of cigarette smoke. The haze cleared to reveal Jennifer and her husband locked in a compromising position on the sofa.

"Oh dear," said Mummy retreating rapidly and modestly shutting the kitchen door after her. "They seem to have made up."

When Jennifer and Charlie presented themselves some seconds later she lost her head completely and flung her arms round Charlie in a maternal embrace. Daddy bounded for the outside loo in case she made him kiss Charlie too. No one remarked that Charlie's flies were undone and Jennifer's shirt was buttoned up wrong. Mummy, parrot-like, kept repeating, "How marvellous to see you, Charlie," and "Go and get that nice bottle of sherry your father has hidden in the outside loo, Helen." Sherry is the Derryrose code word for Banana Wine. Mummy is cute enough to siphon the banana wine into old sherry bottles. Then she feeds the residue to Twinkle.

"Of course you will stay to lunch." She ignored Jennifer's protests, attached herself to Charlie, propelled him from scullery to sitting room. A splash of paraffin, from a handy bottle in the stick box, encouraged the sulky fire to blaze. Then out she raced to the scullery to find something to feed him with, dragging me minus the sherry bottle with her. We opened a dozen tins of beef stew that were being saved until the bomb dropped and heated them up in Twinkle's saucepan.

It was just after dinner that he phoned again – Brian from BMA, the guy who had phoned that other time wanting me to be a model. Was I busy tomorrow? he wanted to know – he had a client for me. And next weekend there was a show on in Slane Castle – but maybe that wasn't my type of modelling.

He puzzled me. If he was a dirty pervert, why was there no deep breathing and stuff like that? Why did he sound pleasant and articulate and plausible?

"That man," I said, "Brian from BMA. It was him on the telephone. He says he's coming to pick me up tomorrow for a modelling job in Belfast. And he's going to phone me again this afternoon to confirm it."

"Oh him," said Mummy, "he has phoned a couple of times but you were never in. I phoned BMA myself one day and they say he's a weirdo."

I felt like my stomach had fallen out of the bottom of my body and irrationally burst into tears.

"Right," said Daddy, "if that phone rings once more today I'm going to answer it and tell that pervert to eff off." Daddy suffers irritable phases on the same days as Mummy, "And if he turns up here tomorrow I'll shoot him."

All afternoon Mummy monopolised Charlie, anxiously making him feel welcome and Daddy sat to attention, his new reading glasses perched fiercely on his forehead, yelling at everyone to keep the sitting-room door open so he could listen for the telephone. I cowered in my bedroom pretending to read *Emily's Quest*, taking guilty gulps of Jennifer's brandy that she had been hiding to help her sleep.

What was I so afraid of? Being afraid, I think. He hadn't even said anything frightening to me.

"Oh pull yourself together, Helen," Jennifer said kindly when she came up to pack to go home with Charlie, "you have to be more confrontational."

But she left me the bottle of brandy and I practised saying "Helen Gordon here. Who's speaking please?" in an aggressive voice, and blaming Mummy for beating all my aggressive tendencies out of me.

Downstairs I could hear Mummy yelling, "I don't care who is ringing. I'm never going to answer the phone again, Kenneth."

She brought me up a fried egg, supervised me while I ate it and wondered loudly why I was so bird-mouthed. But then Linda Patterson had bullied me at Primary School and I'd always been easily led by Laura.

"What is that smell, Helen? I can smell something."

Mummy was convinced it was ketosis, because I am so thin. Letting her do a Biology O Level was a terrible mistake. But Daddy saved me. He smelt my breath and muttered "Brandy", then he examined the bedroom and found six bottles of overripe, reeking elderberry wine.

I used to think Mummy should be put away. When I was fourteen and had no sense of humour I kept a diary recording her sessions of "madness."

None of this was necessary. Brian didn't phone again.

Chapter Ten

"But I don't want to go to Dublin this week, Helen," Laura said, "there's a thousand pounds going at the Take Your Pick in Grubb's Pub on Saturday night."

"I don't want to go either," said Daisy. "I now weigh eleven stone four pounds. There won't be a dress to fit me."

"Please," I said desperately, "please stop being difficult the both of you. Do you think I want to go? To be fitted out as a bridesmaid for Richard Knight's wedding?"

This was emotional blackmail of course, because I was mad to get to Dublin and away from the mystery caller and Mummy's nagging about how thin I was. She sent me to the doctor's this morning for a "tonic and a talking to." Our doctor is Dr Hennessy, alias Anto the Onion who at school stalked me out at Christmas parties for mistletoe kisses. How fascinating that Anto the Medical Doctor has not yet found a cure for his Soft Boiled Eyes. And he still wears a vest. But I'm being cruel. I had a hideous interview with Anto, Dr Hennessy. Mummy probably had him tutored about what he was to say to me. Anto was always putty in my mother's hands. He thinks she's a lovely woman. The first thing he said was, "Helen Gordon, I'd hardly have recognised you." And from Anto, who loved me as a chubby spot-ridden adolescent, this was not a compliment. He examined everything that it is legal for a male doctor to examine unsupervised. I'm not even anaemic, but how could I be with the amount of draught Guinness I drink? It must have been disappointing for both himself and my mother that everything is functioning normally. Mummy wasn't discouraged. She is now convinced that the "problem" is my mind.

So I was mad to get to Dublin to Elisabeth with her alley-cat morals. It would be nice to see Richard too. He was leaving the bogs especially to see us.

"Richard is leaving the bogs especially to see us."

"Oh well," said Laura in what could only be described as a bitchy voice, "well, if the knightly Sir Richard is prepared to give us an audience we'd all better be there to receive him."

Laura has never liked Richard for some reason.

Loyally Daisy said, "I'd love to see Richard. He was always such a friend at UCD." Daisy retreats into religious symbolism when she's feeling sentimental.

" OK," I cheered up, "and I would like to go before my new hairstyle goes native again."

Daddy, learning that my mind was affected, had suggested I go and get my hair done. So I would be safely out of the house should Brian arrive and out of the line of fire when Daddy shot him. He even pressed a fiver into my hand and told me to spend the change on sweeties. It has been a long time since Daddy went to the hairdresser.

"Yes," said Laura snidely, "Richard is guaranteed to notice the root perm with three rollers at the front of your head to give the hair a bit of a lift. It will probably be the first thing he says to you – 'Congratulations on the root perm, Helen. It's a great job'."

Laura's tantrum had nothing to do with Richard Knight. Daisy and I had visited to discuss Operation Bridesmaid and had walked in on herself and Willie having a slanging match about toilet roll. Willie was accusing her of extravagance. "And she's such a little princess," he had complained, "that she won't use newspapers like the rest of us."

"*The Sun* is not a newspaper," Laura snorted contemptuously, "it's a comic."

You know the way when people marry "up" they try to disguise their lowly origins with an artificial display of gentility? Laura, perversely, has been doing the same since she yoked herself to Willie. Laura loves *The Sun*, it's a family institution. Daddy used to dream of recovering the Gordon fortunes by doing *The Sun* Bingo. The papers were saved for Laura coming home from university at weekends to keep her amused when she eventually got out of bed. And when she had them devoured they went into the outside loo to meet the same fate as Willie's.

"I'm sorry I'm not my usual good company," Willie apologised as he pulled on his wellies to go back out to his chickens, "When I got down to the chicken houses this morning the spout had come off the meal bin and there was six tons of meal lying in the yard. And when I came back to get Princess Marigold here to help me shovel it up she just rolled over in bed and asked me if it was insured."

"Ah, poor Willie," Laura suddenly repented and flung herself on him, making the mobile shake in the process. Willie pushed her away. "I'm not really in the mood for a bit of tongue, Laura."

"I should think, Laura," I told her haughtily, "that you would relish a couple of days away from Willie and his guttersnipe ways."

"Oh, if I go Willie is coming with me," said Laura firmly. "We are going to take Roger and camp outside Elisabeth 'Bitchy

Boots's' house in Mount Merrion. Willie and I don't choose to associate with the likes of you."

"You can't go to the Pick Your Pick anyway on Saturday night, Laura," Daisy added persuasively, "Mummy is organising a family party for the new bungalow and she expects us all to be at it."

The most annoying thing about family parties in our family is that all the family come to them. All that inter-in-law bickering is forgotten the minute there is a mention of a big feed. I have been telling her for years that if she stopped going overboard with turkey and stuffing and started dialling a pizza there would be a marked decrease in the numbers who invite themselves along. Aunt Sarah and Mummy haven't spoken to each other since Gran-Gran died when Aunt Sarah accused Mummy of laughing at the funeral, but Aunt Sarah's appetite has never suffered because of it. Daddy is terrified of family parties because Aunt Sarah always says, "Kenneth, I declare you are getting fatter," without fail when she greets him. And Mummy without fail puts him on a diet afterwards. At the last party Uncle Reggie wore a shellsuit and was so well on he spilled his beer over himself and Aunt Sarah (rendered helpless after four glasses of gooseberry wine served from a champagne bottle), screeched with laughter and said everyone would think he had wet himself.

"Oh, Mother has made it clear that she doesn't want me. She thinks Aunt May will boycott the bungalow if I attend. Aunt May won't eat off the same table as an adulteress."

When we got back home Mummy was nursing Twinkle and pretending to study in a chair in front of the range – only she is allowed to sit with her feet in the oven – listening to *These Are The Days Of Our Lives* which she has played endlessly since

Freddie Mercury died. Freddie has replaced *The Quiet Man* in Mummy's heart. "Poor Freddie, and he spoke so nicely."

"Helen, where have you been? That man phoned again."

"What man? The pervert with the dirty phone-calls?"

"No. The man from the Department of Agriculture. He wants to give you a job."

"Educating adolescent boys?"

"Not quite. Some temporary surveying post, or something. I was so engrossed in my Reproduction though, I didn't really listen."

"You are not allowed to listen to Freddie Mercury when you are studying," I scolded her severely. "You promised. It's no wonder you failed the photosynthesis test last week. You never listen to a word I say, Mummy."

"Don't nag, Helen. Me learning about reproduction is a formality. I should be teaching it. Go and phone that nice man and tell him you will take the job."

The Department of Agriculture wanted me for ten weeks, starting January, to survey part-time farmers and find out why none of them took Short Courses at Agricultural Colleges. I had no choice but to accept, not with Mummy breathing fire and encouragement down my neck. But I would rather have had a temporary post modelling milking aprons and wellington boots.

"I think," said Mummy, "that you need some agricultural training before you take that job. Get and do the milking with Daisy, Helen, and send your father in to me. It's against my feminist principals but I need help to put up a pine ceiling in the bathroom of the brown and white bungalow."

I sighed loudly. I had wanted to devote my evening to writing.

My Novel That I Wrote, *Chain Reaction*, had been accepted by the first publishing house I sent it to. But I haven't written anything worth reading since. The sequel to *Chain Reaction* was quite dreadful and got burnt in the range one day in a fit of passion. And my latest effort is so boring I can't bear to look at it any more. Maybe Mummy is right about books. Anyone can write one novel. The country is full of first-time novelists.

In a boiler-suit, in the milking parlour, ruminating on why I had decided to read for a degree in agriculture. Must have been striding romantically through summer meadows at the time. I certainly was not in a December milking parlour with feet like blocks of ice and only Daisy's woolly hat rivalling mine in its silliness.

What an unglamorous job this is, I thought, what a hefty heaving rough hallion of a job. I don't want this job.

In my fifteen minutes of fame as a novelist I had made television appearances and had professional photographs taken. The local papers had interviewed me – "Local Girl Makes Good". That was the life I was born to, even if the television had only been children's television and they wouldn't let me wear my low-cut red and blue shirt because the blue would interfere with the microcosmic background. Wardrobe considerately fitted me out in a vile green alternative. It was probably a ploy to prevent me corrupting impressionable minds. Nervously I had pulled the head off a wart during the interview and it had bled profusely and rather than mop it up with the snot green shirt I had said, "Cut, cut, I'm bleeding to death," on live television.

Fortunately Mummy had fluffed up the videoing and taped the wrong channel so we have no record of my momentous "Cut, cut, I'm bleeding to death."

The Herald serialised *Chain Reaction*, a chapter a week for twenty weeks. My public demanded more Helen Gordon works of creative art so the editor asked me to contribute regularly. At that stage if I had written recipes my Magherafelt fan club would have said they were literary masterpieces. It wasn't long, of course, before creating became more effort than inspiration. I used to make trips to places like the Sperrin Heritage Centre and school speech days to glean ideas. I am particularly proud of one speech day fashion report, having copied all of the fashion bits out of *Hello* magazine.

Those were the days. As I now lack the discipline to concoct a whole story I have taken to contributing pieces of poetry. My poetry is comfortably second rate – most of it rhymes, but *The Herald* editor is eternally supportive and describes it as "approachable" and sticks it in unfilled pages as a stopgap.

I rather fancy *The Herald* editor and if he wasn't married with six children I could be tempted to mix business with pleasure.

Mummy always proof-reads my final draft in case she discovers something scandalous, or libellous, or a naughty word. Once I wrote a story called *Slave to the Scales* about a woman who went on a diet and whose husband complained about the "health shit" she was feeding him. Mummy made me change "health shit" to "rabbit food."

CHAPTER ELEVEN

Elisabeth took one look at Roger and I knew Willie was socially dead by the time she said, "What a sweet little van." But she fixed her smile and shook his hand and if she wiped her own afterwards nobody noticed. Elisabeth is abominable but she has almost enough breeding to hide it.

"Of course you can camp in Roger," she trilled, "but maybe you should camp him in the garage. I know the neighbours."

Willie, who did not realise he was being socially exterminated, said "Thanks love," and I overheard him telling Laura that Elisabeth had a great ass as he reversed Roger in out of sight. But Laura's lazy eyes were blazing. Laura can spot a snub from "Bitchy Boots" at twenty paces.

"God, Richard," she said when we got into the flat, "I recognise that tie. You got it free with the bubble bath, didn't you?" She shouldn't have taken her contempt for the Rich Bitch out on Richard. It was Elisabeth's Anglo-Irish face that needed slapping.

Richard laughed. "I see motherhood hasn't diluted the acid on your tongue, Laura," he said, and handed her a very stiff gin which she pretended she didn't want, but drank anyway.

"This drinks party we've been asked to," Elisabeth balanced herself elegantly on the arm of Richard's chair and smoothed her party frock down over her thighs, "it's a last minute affair but we couldn't really refuse. Why don't we meet you later in Quality Street?"

"Better still," said Richard, "why don't you come with us? Fleur won't mind, and we could all go on to Quality Street together. I'll lend you a bubble bath tie, Willie, if you haven't brought one with you."

"Dead on," Willie put his feet up on the sofa and belched loudly. "But I'll just rest myself here for ten minutes first. Give us another beer would you, Elisabeth, if you are going out to the kitchen."

Laura sighed loudly, "I'm not much in the mood to hob and nob with your friends, Richard, thanks all the same. And I left my party frock at home."

"Of course we will go," I said firmly. I adore drinks parties, having developed the talent years ago of artfully positioning myself beside the drinks cabinet and away from the conversation. "Fleur makes marvellous punch. She's your cousin or something isn't she, Richard?"

Richard and I used to go to Fleur's drinks parties together when we were at UCD. They were the only parties Richard went to willingly. And only because he too could hide beside the drink.

"His cousin?" Elisabeth had returned with Willie's beer and a glass of red wine for me. I can't drink the white stuff anymore, not the cheap white stuff anyway. It gives me indigestion. "Fleur is Richard's sister, Helen, though being a nice boy he doesn't talk about it."

"Sorry darling," she smiled unpleasantly over at Richard and posed gracefully in front of the fireplace, "I've dropped you in it, haven't I?"

"Only a half sister," Richard glowered.

"Yes," Elisabeth laughed dangerously, "an accident in your father's misspent youth, wasn't she?"

Laura thawed out immediately. "In that case," she announced magnificently, "I should be delighted to go to your sister's party. I never knew you had skeletons in your family cupboard, Richard."

Fleur's drawing-room was packed with navy sports coats and Brown Thomas party dresses. From the crescendo of conversation that hit us as we went in, the party had been swinging for some time. So I performed my quickstep manoeuvre immediately and got into position beside the punch-bowl. Fleur always has her drinks table between the bay window and the grand piano so if you sit in the window seat you are well hidden and therefore well protected from the masses. Willie and the girls were not so cute. From my corner I heard Fleur introduce them, via Richard, to her husband who was magnificently robed in a blue velvet smoking jacket.

"Friends of Richard?" he boomed jovially, "you must have read agriculture with him then, William?" Daisy spoke in a small defiant voice, "Actually it was me who read Agricultural Science with Richard."

When Daisy is wearing her Jigsaw dress you would never guess she farmed for a living.

"Creature of habit, aren't you?" Richard's voice floated through the brocade curtain. "Do you need your punch glass filled?"

"Only if you are subtle about it," I passed the glass out to him, "and if you could pass me in another vol-au-vent I would be eternally grateful."

"Pass you in a vol-au-vent," he repeated and performed his practised side step manoeuvre. He joined me in the window seat with a tray of vol-au-vents and two tumblers full of punch.

"God, Helen, you have surpassed yourself this time. You don't usually read a magazine when you are hiding."

"Couldn't resist. It was waiting for me in the bedroom when I went up to take off my coat. Your sister's party is swinging."

He frowned and took a swig of his punch.

"Bit low of Elisabeth to rat like that," I apologised for her, "but really you shouldn't have invited us when it was obvious that she didn't want us. You can't blame her. We were hardly dressed for the occasion."

"She knows as well as I do that you always carry a party frock with you when you go anywhere, Helen."

How true. It's one of the little rules of my disjointed life. Parties often spring up out of nowhere and it is essential to be prepared for them. A party frock is never hard to pack, not the ones I wear anyway.

"And I've trained Daisy to do the same," I grinned. "Never managed to train Laura though. She hasn't taken those high-heeled ankle boots off since Willie bought them for her."

Laura and Willie were helping themselves to punch beside us.

"Where is that tart Helen?" Laura was scolding, "she has my cigarettes in her bag. I suppose she has found herself a man already and has dragged him off to have her wicked way with him."

"It's a possibility I suppose," Willie's voice floated in. "How long are Elisabeth and Richard engaged, Laura?"

"Couple of months."

"Funny they never grope each other. They don't even hold hands. That Elisabeth has a desperate sharp tongue, hasn't she?"

The voices floated off and I said, "You'd better grope her a bit more often in front of Willie, Richard, or he will be suggesting marriage guidance for you next."

He didn't answer me. He is infuriating that way.

"The path of true love never ran straight," I comforted. "Are you nearly ready to brave the party again and get us more punch?"

"There is no such thing as true love," Richard stood up and took my tumbler, "it's all compatibility."

Elisabeth nabbed him by the punch-bowl.

"Richard, darling," Elisabeth's voice is awfully posh. I could never mistake her for anyone else. "Can we leave soon for Quality Street? That Willie Simpson person has now kissed everybody in the room, men also. When I last passed him he was asking Christopher if he knew anyone who had a drive shaft for a Mark 2 Escort for his stock car."

"Christopher, my sister's husband?"

"You deserved that, darling. The Gordons are super girls but it's hard to excuse Willie Simpson as eccentric when it's so obvious he's only common. I'm sure you have poor Helen hidden away somewhere, Richard. Do fetch her and we'll go. Poor Helen, she has got so thin. Perhaps she is pining away for you, darling."

"Don't be such a bitch, Elisabeth."

"I love you too, darling."

I used to go to Quality Street a lot as a student when I got bored being a student. You can wear tiny dresses to Quality Street and take a taxi home. To be convincing in the Faculty of Agriculture you have to wear jeans and use your bicycle for transportation. I should have realised then that I wasn't cut out to be an Ag. Quality Street always has rich young Arabs with apartments in Ballsbridge and credit cards to buy champagne.

Elisabeth and I usually tackled Quality Street together because the rich young Arabs invariably had a taste for white girls and champagne at the same time.

"You and Elisabeth used to come here, didn't you?" Richard and I were dancing to Sinead O'Connor's *Nothing Compares To U*. I have always enjoyed dancing with him because he holds me very tight and doesn't feel embarrassed about it. Beside us Willie was wrapped around Elisabeth, and I swear to God she was enjoying it.

"We did. That was my Outrageous phase. Red slit dress and hair all round my face."

"Finished up the wine and fell all over the place. Elisabeth thinks you have got thin, Helen."

"I heard her. It is as well you are engaged to her then. You have always preferred a big woman to hold on to."

"You and Richard look so well dancing together, Helen," Daisy said in the Ladies where she was having a private cigarette. Daisy would die rather than smoke in front of Richard, whom she idolises.

"I suppose so," I took a little puff myself. "You know what they say about dancing being the vertical expression of a horizontal desire. Or whatever it is. Was Elisabeth always such a bitch, Daisy?"

"Oh yes, but never to us before. She was unspeakably rude to Willie at Fleur's party, but somebody had to stop him telling that terrible story about the fox on holiday. He told Fleur he ate it with onions. Then he stuck his hand down her shirt when we were leaving. I can't really blame Elisabeth this time. That would embarrass anybody."

"Fleur deserved it. She is the most horrible superior snob I've ever met. Aunt Maisie is a pussy cat in comparison. All those bloody questions about who you are and where you come from."

We had failed with Fleur immediately. She didn't like pretty girls in short dresses.

"I should have worn the fur coat," Daisy stubbed out her cigarette carefully in case she set fire to Quality Street, "and you should have Aunt Maisie's Chanel with you. Stop worrying about Willie's feelings, Helen. Himself and Elisabeth have made up. I noticed her taking a pretty embarrassing grope at him when you were dancing with Richard. Elisabeth always liked a bit of rough. "

It is Daisy's secret regret that Richard and I never made a go of it with each other. I was really keen on him once, it was an adolescent passion for the unobtainable. Daisy used to dream that we would be shipwrecked together on a desert island and he would declare himself. Sometimes I used to dream the same thing myself. Now I would expect true love and life happy ever after, clichéd and all as it is. I am not satisfied with compatibility.

Elisabeth was still dancing with Willie when we returned and Laura was suffering a bad attack of jealousy grumps.

"I knew it was a crap idea, going to a party with that pair. You were so keen to get to it, Helen, yet I didn't see you once when we got there. And look at that dirty tart Elisabeth. She's all over Willie and he's loving it. Manipulating cow. He is that stupid he can't see through her."

Echoes of someone else. Jennifer?

"You know," said Laura magnificently, "I almost feel sorry for Richard, yoked to her. I know he used you in the same way at UCD, Helen, but still she would be a heavy passenger to take through life with you."

"Richard will be OK," I sighed. "He doesn't believe in true

love, just compatibility. And he didn't use me at UCD, Laura. We were only friends. We weren't joined at the hip."

"You were always a soft touch," Laura commented as Richard returned from the bar with a generous glass of gin for her. If the way to Daisy's heart is through her stomach, the way to Laura's is via a gin bottle. Hence that whisper of sympathy for Richard's heavy passenger.

CHAPTER TWELVE

Because I am a structured person I will not excuse Richard's seduction as an impulsive action. I have been scheming for years to shift Richard. When we were at UCD an anonymous shift on a sweaty dance floor would have satisfied me. But as you get older horizons broaden, ambitions intensify and close dancing is no longer enough.

So I reflected anyway as I lay in his fiancée's house that night trying to sleep once we got home from Quality Street. Next door he lay in his fiancée's bed. Soon they would be married and I would still be scheming to shift him.

Impulsive actions are never really spontaneous. I think they are premeditated in the subconscious and preserved till the time is right.

"So how are we going to organise this?"

Elisabeth, Daisy, Richard and I were breakfasting on Bucks Fizz and croissants, like Beautiful People. Laura and Willie, we presumed, were brewing tea below us in the campervan.

"Why don't we all take a bus into town together and the girls can take it in turns to be fitted?" Richard suggested reasonably.

"Wonderful organisation, darling," Elisabeth yawned elegantly. "And whoever is fitted out first can help you choose your Christmas presents, Richard. I haven't the energy to plod round shops today."

What could have been simpler?

"I suggest you get fitted out first then, Helen," Richard smiled across the table at me, "we used to have great fun Christmas shopping together when we were at UCD."

He must have said that to irritate Elisabeth. We only shopped once together, years ago, and I had blisters on my feet for a week afterwards. We hadn't even stopped for lunch. But he and Elisabeth had had a futile argument about the Bucks Fizz glasses just after we got up. Richard had insisted on washing them because they were dusty. Then he wouldn't let us drink out of them immediately because he judged them still too warm to "appreciate" it. He has a real knack for winding up Elisabeth.

"Laura and Willie and I thought we'd go to see *Dances With Wolves*, Elisabeth," Daisy offered, "would you like to come with us?" Since Elisabeth's performance the previous evening Daisy was afraid to be left alone with her. Daisy was never a match for Bitchy Boots.

Elisabeth and I have always had similar tastes and I liked the Pre-Raphaelite bridesmaid's dresses. My creative eye appreciates the outrageous romanticism of billowing tulle skirts, scattered roses and gold embroidery. Surprising though that Daisy, the artist among us, did not agree.

"These are fashion mistake dresses," she whispered confidentially, "Laura and I will look like tanks in all these frills."

"Maybe a little grotesque," I agreed, "I look like the poisoned dwarf in a pantomime. She must plan to make us as ugly as possible so she looks stunning."

We giggled. "Did you see the monstrosity she's going to wear? 'Bride of Frankenstein'. I've never seen anything like it. Johnboy wouldn't marry me if I turned up in an outfit like that. He'd stop the whole show and tell me to go home and change into something that gave me a figure."

"I thought Johnboy said you hadn't a tight enough grip on reality to be married to him?"

"Oh, that was last month."

Richard and I rendezvoused in Bewley's on George's Street. In our friendship days it was convenient to the charity shops and second-hand bookstores. If one was late, the other had plenty to occupy himself with.

"No presents bought yet?"

He was doing the *Irish Times* crossword.

"Do you want another cup of tea?"

I hate it when he doesn't answer me. But I'm used to it.

"I'd rather have a drink," he stood up, "coming?" And he strode out towards the door, not even glancing back to check I was following. Laura is right. I am a Soft Touch. I followed. I should have sat my ground in Bewley's but then I never would have seduced him.

"Richard," I said crossly, "why do you always assume that I'm going to follow you? I would never stride ahead into a pub and expect you to come after me. Very presumptuous of you having a drink sitting waiting for me."

"Please Helen, don't start that liberated woman stuff with me. Sit down and drink your beer like a good girl."

I sat down and sulked a bit at his patronising tone. Sometimes there's a strong family resemblance to Fleur. But I drank the beer. Richard ignored the tiny protest.

"What's wrong with you?" I asked eventually. I had bought a second round and grown tired of trying to complete the crossword. He was reading the Death Notices, checking that no one had died who he had to buy a Christmas present for.

"Richard, shithawk, answer me, what's wrong with you?"

Forget shifting and seduction. Richard needs his bum

soundly smacked.

"Very well then. You don't want to talk about it." Two glasses of beer at lunchtime do funny things to my head. Extraordinary potency. Make me tough enough to say things that are better left unsaid. Probably.

"I know damn well what's wrong with you. If you don't want to marry her, break off the engagement. Marrying Elisabeth won't make you different."

"I have no idea what you are talking about." He didn't even bother lifting his head from the Death page.

"Yes you do," I snapped, cross for some reason. "I can read you like a book. You always use me like a life jacket when something goes wrong. God knows, Richard, you used to make me decipher your lecture notes when you couldn't read them at university. Damn sight more than you ever did for me. Any of the really big things in my life, you have run away from them."

"Don't be hysterical, Helen. You could never hold your drink at lunch-time."

I pouted. "Sticks and stones may break my bones, Richard. Extraordinary how I never noticed the family resemblance with Fleur before. Please stop taking your shaky love life out on me. It's awfully boring."

I went to the bar to get us both a drink – a stiff one for myself. Lunch-time drinks do make me giddy, yet because Richard always excuses drinking conversation as drunken conversation, I could say what I wished with little chance of having it flung back in my face.

Richard was smiling when I returned. He must have decided to behave.

"Sorry to bore you, Helen. I never thought you minded."

I stuck my nose in the air, "Don't start apologising to me now and break the habit of a lifetime. I will be starting to think you are getting soft." I didn't want to forgive him, but I always get sucked in when he smiles.

"Do tell, Richard," I asked, "what is it like marrying someone you aren't in love with? Being incurably romantic myself I wouldn't know. It isn't a mortal sin is it?"

"I told you I don't believe in love."

"I know, you said it was all compatibility. Is Elisabeth compatible with your mummy? Does Fleur think she's suitable? Do you think compatible people can be happy?"

Happiness was a horrible word to throw at him. Nobody knows if they will be happy. I'm not. Richard probably will be most happy. Love makes people insecure and irritable and pathetic.

Anyway his happiness was no concern of mine. We weren't intimate friends, just sparring partners with lustful designs. In my Tart days I had tried to seduce him but he wisely fought me off. It would have been a sign of weakness to display human feelings. I am as closed up as he is.

Just after university I had a brain haemorrhage. Richard didn't come to see me though I was in hospital for weeks. I didn't expect him to come when I was in Intensive Care but I have never really forgiven him for it. If he had been dying I would have flown to Timbuktu to be with him.

I blurted it out. Unlike Richard I know that drunks are responsible for every word they utter. And to hell with the consequences.

"Why did you not come to see me when I was dying that time?"

He was appalled. I had said the wrong thing. I was only trying to get a reaction. Our banter was nosediving. Two things you should never do to a man – rake up his past and ask him what he thinks of you.

Richard backed into his high tower.

"Please don't drag up the past so viciously, Helen. Your greatest charm was always the way you left things unsaid. Wringing deathbed confessions out of a man was never your style."

I was ashamed of myself. But isn't it true that once you start digging a hole you usually dig yourself in deeper?

"I said that you always run away from the big things in my life," I said evenly. "I'm tired of pussyfooting around, Richard. We are dancing in circles as usual. On your deathbed you will be thinking of yourself as usual. I will be the last thing on your mind."

And Jennifer and Mummy say I can't be confrontational.

Richard panicked. "Stop, Helen. Stop blaming me. You were always a scheming and manipulating witch. You would have crucified me if I had ever given in to you. Wham bam thank you mam. And on to the next victim."

I was in control at last. I said, "You wouldn't have suffered. You don't even believe in true love, you are unaffectionate, unfeeling and cold."

He was angry. He blustered, "Sticks and stones may break my bones..."

I tired suddenly of the argument because it was pointless and thoughtfully took a handful of his sweater. And I kissed him. We had never kissed before, since the one occasion I tried to seduce him. I doubt we had even touched. This was no peck on the lips either. It was a real snog because he kissed me back passionately. Seduction and adrenaline and the element of surprise. Richard's ice had been trying to crack for years. Who cared that now the time was right. I would still respect him in the morning.

"Damn you, Helen." His heart was racing so loud the barflies could probably hear it. I should have done it years ago, just grabbed him and kissed him. Instead of flirting and scheming and suffering.

Richard becomes very masterful in the throes of passion. "We can't stay here," he announced, lifting our stuff, propelling me outside, holding tight, not letting me away.

"Time for Christmas presents?" I asked, disappointed. Was he freezing up again? So soon?

He kissed me. I made sure my hands slid under his sweater and touched him. If my moment of victory was only going to be a moment I wanted proper memories to remember.

"In the present circumstances," his voice was lost in my hair, "not a very bright idea, Christmas presents."

We went to the pictures, one that wasn't showing *Dances With Wolves*. We sat in the double seats at the back and for the first time in my life, I think, I never saw the film. Worse. I couldn't even tell you what it was called.

All those people who shift at the pictures – is it because they have nowhere else to go either? Is it the subtle charm of getting tangled in a double seat? Or the wonderful sensitivity of darkness?

The Christmas streets were crammed with shoppers. Everyone was laughing and jostling and pushing. Richard forged a passage through them to the bus stop and held me tight while we waited.

"You can't take me back to Elisabeth's house. I don't want to go back. What if they are already home?"

Then it would all be over.

"Shit shit shit. She hasn't left the spare key."

He bundled me in through the garage window at the back. The door up into the house was locked but with typical disregard for law and order, the back door of Roger was lying open to the world.

We climbed inside. It was left lying as Willie and Laura had left it. The roof was up and the bed above the cab was rumpled. To her credit Laura insists on blankets and refuses to sleep in a bag. The kitchen table was still scattered with breakfast things.

"Will we sit up on the bed and wait for them, Richard?"

Richard shut Roger's back door, smiling.

"Yes, we'll sit up on the bed and wait for them."

CHAPTER THIRTEEN

It was awful, the first day. I knew I wasn't going to be happy the moment I arrived and an officious little man told me to move the motorbike, it was illegally parked in a reserved bit of carpark. He wasn't even nice about it.

"Come on, sonny, move it before I call security." I was more annoyed that he thought I was male.

We didn't even do any surveying. We got to know each other. I hate this sort of interaction stuff, playing group games and drinking coffee. Together. My partner was picking his nose with orange loo roll when we were introduced but I still recognised him. Burgundy Balls. On a school trip to France years ago he had everything from his face cloth to his underpants burgundy. We know about the underpants because the other boys ripped his burgundy shorts off him and we saw. And it was the first time I ever saw tackle. That's how I remember.

We were paired off to delve into each other's personalities. There are two types of men in the world. Those I can manipulate and those who manipulate me. I flirt with the former and we chat endless triviality. But the latter don't appreciate small talk. They touch with me and I crumble. They yell at me and I cry. They talk to me and I listen.

I couldn't even recall Burgundy Ball's name. Jonathan, Jeremy, Jason, Jemima?

His name was James. Of course. How could I have forgotten? And though he was not colour co-ordinated that day he giggled behind a limp white hand when I told him I had come on a motorbike. Sure how else was I going to get there? It was very decent of Willie to lend it. Willie and I have been great friends since we were in Dublin before Christmas and he discovered Richard and I in the campervan together. Not the first time when we were drinking tea in a very platonic manner, but the next day when we were making more than tea.

All that fun with Richard is a blank now. It was sparkle and brightness and beauty at the time, having fun, but nothing afterwards. Himself and Elisabeth are getting married in the middle of March. Elisabeth phoned to tell us. I'm going to have to take a couple of days off work. She says Richard is sending a letter to ask us what we want as presents. I never realised that the bridegroom was supposed to buy the bridesmaids something. I hope he doesn't expect me to reply. I don't think it's a good idea for him and me to communicate anymore.

"Did you knock them out, Helen?"

"I have this boy, Willie, called James. He is one of the manipulated type. He is worse. He is the type of boy who tucks his vest into his burgundy underpants."

"I bet Richard Knight never did a thing like that."

"Willie, get on the bike and shut up. That is supposed to be our little secret."

I'm never sure about Willie, whether he can be manipulated or trusted or not. One minute I think I've got him sussed and the next he is beyond categorisation.

"I promised I wouldn't tell," said Willie staunchly, "I know what happens when people break promises. Colin told me yesterday. God writes their name in his Black Book in pen. I wish you would let me tell Laura. You know how she loves a bit of dirt."

"No, Willie."

Laura would be livid if she found out It had happened. She has always chastised me for being putty in Richard's hands. She says I was never fit for him, I'm too soft.

"I never thought you would sink so low as to fall for a married man, Helen," Willie pulled on his helmet in a huff, "and you always mooning on about romance. He can hardly leave her yet. They aren't even married."

What is the world coming to when Willie Simpson can justifiably lecture me on morality?

I poked him, "Willie, you self-righteous pig, you are living with a married woman. And for the record, Willie, they will have to stay married. There's no divorce in Ireland."

Every year at Derryrose we go through a foreign holiday phase. There is a blink of sun and someone starts to fantasise about the sun and sea and sand, and before you know it, Laura is telling you sex is rampant in hot countries – all those men with no clothes on – she says it's a difficult choice, the blushing Irish boy or the randy native.

"Laura," I said, "you have never been on a foreign holiday."

"And I have never seen a blushing Irish boy either."

Daisy had been into Magherafelt looking for honeymoon destinations. She originally wanted Georges V in Paris for a week with lunch in Maxim's every day, then decided on Goa in India because the brochure said that in five years' time smart people would be talking about it at cocktail parties. After initially saying, "It looks dirty," I had to agree with her that even if they did use the beaches as toilets she didn't have to tell Johnboy until they got there.

And she has been trying to organise The Church. Daisy does not consider Magherafelt Presbyterian aesthetically pleasing for a wedding. Certainly the wall behind the pulpit is an extraordinary colour, some would call it "diarrhoea". Daisy has discussed this with Reverend Robinson, who assures her that short of an Act of God the colour cannot be changed on the whim of one communicant member. Daisy is now driving around the country searching for a suitable church even though Reverend Robinson has advised her that normal people get married in their own church.

"Did you have a good time today, Helen?" She was undecided between Udaipurs Lake Palace Hotel built in 1628 by the Maharanees of Mewer as a summer retreat and the Ladshadweep Islands where they dropped you off from a boat and didn't come back to collect you for a week.

"No, it was horrible, and I have been paired off with Burgundy Balls."

"James? Has he turned out nice-looking?"

"No." I lifted a brochure of Crete. "Johnboy won't like it here, Daisy, there are no pictures of topless women."

"It was Sarah who wanted Crete actually. She has been teaching her class about Minoan civilisations. Helen, there must have been something nice about James."

"Daisy, when I need a matchmaker, I will ask you."

Daisy ignored the snub. "Why don't you and Sarah go to Crete together? And do a Shirley Valentine," she suggested. "You haven't been out of the house since Christmas. Mummy nearly had to kidnap you to get you to her housewarming party."

"And wasn't I the star once I got there?"

I had employed all resources to escape the family housewarming. First I hid in Derryrose and told Daisy to say I was sick. Mummy came and fetched me so I offered to stay in the kitchen and supervise the turkey as a compromise. Then I offered to do the washing up, which should have pleased her, but she was showing off and said they would use the dishwasher. We won that dishwasher in a raffle once, but Mummy never used it – she said she already had five dishwashers, and the machine seized in protest. Then I told her I was tired. Nothing worked. I joined the family to play "How Many Things Can You Do With A Plastic Bag?".

"Did anyone else think of using it to carry goldfish and bury bombs?"

Crete did sound interesting. Particularly the national poteen, called raki, which they claimed separated the men from the boys. That would be handy to know.

"Oh Helen, I nearly forgot, there's a letter for you from Richard in the hall."

"How do you know it's from Richard, Daisy, did you open it?"

Not that it would really have mattered if she did. I was willing to bet money he hadn't even signed it "Love Richard."

"Of course not. But Richard still has the dirtiest envelopes in the world."

"You know, Daisy," I said unreasonably, firing the Crete brochure off the wall and storming into the kitchen to cut the blue mould bits off the cheese and make myself a sandwich, "if you bring up the subject of Richard Knight getting married once more I swear I will run away. I never got presents from Lee and Charlie when I did bridesmaid for Laura and Jennifer and I've never suffered because of it."

"I thought you didn't mind, Helen, about Richard marrying Elisabeth." Daisy followed me into the kitchen and absent-mindedly began to eat the blue mould. "You said on the way back from Dublin that it was as well they were marrying each other as neither seemed capable of fidelity or true love."

"God, Daisy, my head has been lifting all day. This third degree about Richard Knight isn't helping. I'm going to get a tablet for it."

"No, Helen, don't take another pain-killer," she eased the gully out of my hand as the phone started ringing, "let me massage the back of your neck. Migraines are caused by a build-up of toxins and tensions at the top of the spine."

Daisy and Johnboy had taken a ten-week body massage course at the Tech. Johnboy had hoped it would fuel their love-life, massaging each other's feet and such like. I don't think he was successful, but one thing you must say for Johnboy, he deserves marks for trying.

"I wish you would learn the magic words, Daisy, that take the pain away."

I lifted the phone. It was the mystery caller. A voice like butter. I went into orbit. What Sarah called The Rabbit during Laura-gate was small talk in comparison. My repertoire impressed even me. I was breathless when I slammed the phone down.

Daisy applauded and dug out a bottle of drink. I had done it. I had been confrontational. What a clever clever girl.

"Johnboy and I are booking our wedding reception tonight," Daisy confided.

"Don't tease, Daisy," I poured more poteen, "you have booked it twice already."

There are so many hotels in Magherafelt they prostitute

themselves for business. So if you phone up inquiring about a wedding for two hundred guests, management gets so excited it sends you a Free Feed Voucher. It's not chicken and chips in a basket either. Daisy's last Free Feed was fillet steak stuffed with pâté and surrounded by puff pastry (Beef Wellington, £9.95 on the À La Carte). Of course she had to book her wedding reception as well. Already she is getting married in September '92 and September '93. It's very difficult to get a Saturday in September.

"No one knows the day or the hour," she informed me mysteriously, "Johnboy and I might decide to get married in a hurry."

"Daisy, how can you have a shotgun wedding? You won't even let Johnboy touch your breasts."

"Let's not quibble over technicalities," Daisy grinned, "do you want to know a secret?"

"Johnboy proposed."

"No, not yet, but he suggested as much when he told me the secret. If I tell you, Helen, you must promise not to tell anybody."

"Daisy, stop behaving like we were at Primary School."

"Promise."

"I promise."

"Sandra is pregnant."

"She's not."

"She is. Dr Hennessy confirmed it this morning."

So The Rabbit had begun to breed, to multiply, to populate the earth with lots of other little Rabbits.

"How much longer have we left? Till civilisation as we know it is overrun by little Rabbits?"

"Oh, she is only a couple of weeks pregnant. It was a

Christmas conception. Johnboy says there was too much goodwill served with the brandy butter. Promise again that you won't tell Helen."

"Hardly. I'm more interested in Elisabeth making it to the marriage vows with Richard. I've got a funny feeling one of them might back out."

"Don't you want to know what Johnboy said about us getting married? He said 'Sandra is pregnant, Daisy, but our children will be better looking'."

That evening I read Richard's letter. I really should write back and stop being melodramatic about our encounter. There was no point regretting it now. He wasn't going to leave Elisabeth and run away with me. I didn't want him to anyway. I don't think we would ever be happy together. He had probably forgotten it had ever happened. I was filed away like all the other women he had known. He would never leave Elisabeth. Still, there was no harm in hoping.

CHAPTER FOURTEEN

I knew I was going to be late the moment I woke. I hadn't even time to slap on some foundation. Daisy is right about me being absent-minded. Last night I tried to cleanse my face with nail-polish remover, and cut it to ribbons. I had slept really badly and had a lot of strange wide-awake dreams. I dreamed of Richard, he told me to put pepper in his hot whiskey and I had and he was surprised and kept saying, "She put pepper in it," and his eyes watered. Then I was convinced that Richard was in the room with me and he had photographed me in the dark in bed, and I woke yelling, "Richard you low dog". And then I dreamt I was graduating from UCD again and someone was making a speech and going on and on, and then I woke up and discovered it was actually Radio 4 and I was sleeping through the alarm.

"My friend" James kept me a seat in the Conference Room. He was dolled up in a shiny burgundy suit with no tie. I pushed my biker's helmet under the chair as our lecturer opened with, "Well, without further ado, I will crack on."

I was determined not to be interested. James scribbled endless laborious pages of endless trivial theory until smoke began to come out of his pencil. I tried to compose a suitable letter to Richard. But everything I thought of was either too stiff or too flippant. Anyway I was not totally confident about the tone of his letter. Since we left UCD I doubt Richard has written more than his signature on a cheque book and his ink pen had smudged most of the sentences.

"Who are you writing to?" James inquired as he massaged his burning fingers at the coffee break, 10.30 am sharp, "a boyfriend?"

"My lover," I said, but I could tell he didn't believe me the way he laughed uproariously.

At lunch-time I escaped into the library with a banana concealed in my biker jacket and read *Profitable Sheep Farming* to alleviate the boredom. James had offered to take me into town in his car for a hamburger but I declined, unsure if I could handle the excitement. Anyway I would have died to have been seen out with someone wearing a suit and no tie.

In the library, after a tedious chapter on Stocking Rates, I decided what to do about Richard's letter. I would send a poem to him. Not one of my own, which were depressing of late and cutting rather too close to the bone, but *People* by DH Lawrence. Why should he get a "We had a jolly time, let's forget it now you are marrying" letter to clean his conscience for him?

"I like people quite well at a little distance."

James said he searched the whole of the Conference Centre to find me. Then he remembered I was a novelist. My natural habitat was in the midst of literature. He had liked the dirty bits in *Chain Reaction*, he said, though he usually preferred a book with the picture of a gunman on the front.

James thinks I should stay over in the Conference Centre for this week's training and go out socialising with the other two surveyors. He says they had great crack at the bowling alley last night. It was a moment of weakness, certainly something to do with resolving the "Richard's letter" dilemma, but I said I would.

Mummy will be proud of me. Since Christmas she has been tutoring me in the art of "Surviving at Work". The Golden Rule is "Keep In With Your Colleagues And They Will Cover For You."

I told James that if he took the suit off we could go to Clublands together. He promised to show me a good time, which will be interesting. I might even shift him, if there isn't anybody more exciting to shift instead. When I was at UCD we used to have interminable discussions about shifting one's male friends. Could you still be friends again afterwards? How amusing to think we actually cared. Now I'm sure it's better to have loved and lost. It's time to stop romanticising and fantasising about Richard and get back into routine again.

Wednesday night was a success, though not the way I planned it. I know this sounds un-Helen-like and egotistical but that night I was the farmer's ideal woman. Without blushing I can boast that half of Clublands watched as I walked in with James.

Initially I thought, "Oh no, maybe this cerise, crushed velvet, gynaecologically tight-fitting catsuit was the wrong choice after all," but no, they were openly admiring me. I've never drawn anything like this attention elsewhere.

They were, James said, Ag students from the local college.

"Well, let's go and chat to them," I suggested, "and I can talk to them about reversing tractors and trailers. I can never remember which way to turn the wheel and I've never understood why the damned thing just won't run backwards without swaying all over the place."

"Oh, we can't talk to them," James told me, shocked.

"Why not, James? They look like they are good fun." But then

James had been shocked earlier when I swore at the traffic lights for turning red as we drew up to them.

"They are very rough looking," James said nervously twisting the ring on his little finger, but by then one of them had asked me to dance. He smelled of cows, I like the smell of cows. We did the Timewarp and he told me his name was Dirthead and he'd never seen such a nice pair of legs before, but he'd heard that ginger-haired women had terrible tempers.

James came and took me away at the end of the music. "I thought you needed rescuing," he explained.

"Not at all," I replied airily, "I haven't had so many compliments in my life before."

"He's drunk," said James.

"I know." I rose, "lucky him. Can I get you a drink? We can take a taxi back to the Conference Centre. I can't drink Diet Coke and blackcurrant all night, not with all those farmers standing round looking for a bit of action."

"Just a fizzy orange," said James firmly, "but I don't mind how many drinks you have, Helen."

James was going to regret saying that. I had quite a few because I could tell he contributed to Richard's Theory on Woman and Drink – " A Bit Of Drink And It's Any Port In A Storm".

Thinking about Richard was about as useful as chasing my tail so I went off to dance with another farmer called Macho instead.

"Well, you know, James," I protested when he took me back to the Conference Centre early in his car, "I haven't had so much fun since I was at university. Clublands was always rumoured to have a favourable male to female ratio. Perhaps Sarah and I should forget Crete and launch a strategic campaign on the place to catch husbands. Dirthead and Macho were perfect instruments for my satisfaction. I enjoyed them enormously. Do you know why they call him Dirthead? Because he never washes his hair. I never found out why Macho was called Macho. Do you know?"

"Are you drunk, Helen?"

"Would you be very shocked and refuse to be my surveying partner, James, if I said I was?"

Next morning my mouth tasted like a sewer. I have never tasted a sewer, but I'm hazarding an educated guess. I only had four gin and tonics I think. Usually you can tell the level of my drunkenness by the amount I have written before going to bed. When Laura drinks she becomes obsessed with the telephone and phones the country. Already since she moved in with Willie we have had countless middle of the night emergency phonecalls to Derryrose from her. Sometimes she sets the phone down without speaking, but usually she tells us all how much she loves us and not to worry, she has a sober lift home.

Being more literary than Laura I spill myself into the written word. I have countless dodgy diary entries from university life to pay testimony to the number of big Ag. nights out I was on.

But last night I hadn't bothered with a diary. I'd written a letter to Richard on the fly leaf of *Profitable Sheep Farming*.

> Dear Richard,
>
> I don't care. I'm swaying, maybe the room is spinning, I've dropped my pen, lifted it, resumed. You are so lucky to have found a nice girl, no horsy face, no husky knickers. She won't make gooseberry wine that's poisonous, or fall off when a horse bucks her – she has a family tree and her mother will never want a job folding underwear in Wellworths.

Fortunately enough, the rest of this meandering self-pitying epistle is lost in a drunken scrawl. I ripped the page into tiny shreds. It was worse than dreaming about him. He was getting *People* by DH Lawrence and that was all.

James arrived bearing tea and tablets for my head.

"It's not my head that's sore," I moaned lying prostrated like a fallen woman, "it's my knees. I haven't strutted my funky stuff for so long that they have been damaged. For the past hour and a half we have been arguing, my knees and I. They refuse to bend."

Bravado soon faded. I was hungover, hangdog, hungry. And it wasn't only my knees which ached. My "fallen woman" catsuit was not designed for the female anatomy. I may be permanently scarred where it cut into my cleavage and buttocks.

"God, James, I'm really sorry I was so naughty last night. But I have just ended a traumatic and long term love affair and I'm not back in shape yet."

The manipulated man is easy to apologise to – James forgave me immediately. I didn't even have to grovel. How could I ever respect him?

"I understand so well, Helen. I suffered the pangs of unrequited love once. My heart cracked. I actually heard it. Was it someone you were in Dublin with, Helen?"

"He was actually. Why? Did I tell you the whole sordid story?"

He patted my hand sympathetically. "I'm very discreet, Helen. The night my heart cracked I went to a school rugby disco and drank beer all night. And when my mummy came to take me home I peed in the back seat of the car. No humiliation can rival that experience. The passing years do little to ease my shame. So I can understand your temptation to remember life as wonderful at UCD if the object of your affections shares the memory."

"Alcoholic ramblings, James." I blew my nose on the sheet, astonished by his spontaneous confession. But I didn't have the energy that morning to sympathise with him and his unrequited love.

"It's marvellous how drunks like me can only remember the occasional bits of excitement in the past, isn't it? There were weeks and months of freezing bathrooms and unhoovered carpets and home-made vegetable soup. If I got the chance I would never go back."

Brave words.

"Me neither," James was agreeing, "I got my car stolen once in final year."

"God, James, you must have been very affluent students at Queen's. I only ever had a bicycle. And even now I'm riding a borrowed motorbike."

James tried every means of persuasion, bar That One, but I refused to get out of bed. My knees wouldn't let me. I languished there all day, squeezing out the odd crocodile tear of self-pity. Would it be Crete or Clublands to cure my self-esteem? The charming Macho had advised Crete last night, he thought the sun might even make my breasts grow.

"Jesus, Helen, there are enough alcohol fumes in here to cause an explosion," said Willie, when he came to get me later. "It's a good job I don't fancy you because I think I would stop, the shape you are in. You are really bad looking with no make-up on."

"I only had four gin and tonics," I struggled furiously to my feet, "I've seen you in far worse shape when we were on holiday."

"Go and throw up, Helen, you'll feel better."

I scowled, "Take me home, Willie and stop teasing. I haven't the energy today to steer it."

"Did you shift?"

"No I didn't and one snide comment from you about there being no one to compare with Richard Knight and I'll probably burst into tears and embarrass us both."

Willie and I didn't speak on the way home. If I had had enough energy left over from holding on to him on the back of the bike I might have cried. But it would only have steamed up the visor of my helmet so I didn't bother.

CHAPTER FIFTEEN

"Hello Helen, you look awful, were you drinking gin? What date is your birthday again? I can never remember between you and Daisy."

"How did you know I was drinking gin? It's the twelfth of October."

"You only ever drink gin when you are depressed. The twelfth of October. That makes you a Libran. It says here that Librans are in love with the idea of love and often confuse infatuation with the Real Thing. For them a life without love is not worth contemplating. . . God, Helen, that sounds just like you."

"It does not. And I'm not depressed. I'm just hungover. What are you reading, Laura? Or are you just making it up?"

"*The Zodiac Guide to Love and Sex*. My new Common (no pun intended) Law mother-in-law gave it to me. Did you not know Slack Alice reads teacups? I'm a Leo. That means I'm expansive, generous, caring, passionate and demonstrative."

"And I feel an urge coming on," said Willie. He had changed out of his biker stuff into Mickey Mouse pyjamas and was nursing the twins.

"Make a noise like a turnip, Helen, they like that."

I rose. If whiskers had begun to sprout from my already green face I could not have felt more like a gooseberry. What other urge could Willie be having, wearing those pyjamas?

"Sit down, Helen, and have a cup of tea with us." Laura pushed me back down onto the sofa. She was wearing her Wedding Night Negligée, but then, she rarely changed out of it. "We Leos like nothing more than spoiling our loved ones."

I made a frustrated, embarrassed noise, "Some other time, Laura, OK? I'll go on home and leave the pair of you to let Nature take its course."

"We're not dressed for nookie," Willie laughed, "in bed we dress as Nature intended. I have a matter to discuss with you Helen. I read *Chain Reaction* last night."

Chain Reaction, the silly little novel I wrote while convalescing from my brain haemorrhage. In it the hero was handsome, the villain was ugly and the heroine was a blonde.

"I thought it had a lot of untapped potential," Willie said. You would think Willie knew what he was talking about.

"That's very kind of you, Willie," I told him politely, for novel writing is a sore spot with me, "but you know yourself that any rubbish is published these days. As my charming mother says 'Anyone can write one novel. The country is full of first-time novelists'."

"Well, I'm thinking about writing a novel myself at the minute," Willie confided, "*Confessions of a Chicken Farmer*. These are my Writing Pyjamas. I feel inspired when I wear them."

Laura returned with a loaf of toast and a jar of honey.

"Go for it, Willie," she commanded and before I had one soggy slice worried down, the pair of them had the whole loaf demolished between them.

"Willie and I are writing *Confessions of a Chicken Farmer* between us," Laura explained, "and we use the honey as brain food. Willie thinks of the ideas and I help him with the spellings. We are trying to think of a really good title at the minute. I read somewhere that it's the title that sells sensational novels."

And I would have thought a man with Willie's obvious literary talents and a woman with an A Level in English could produce Booker Prize winning material.

"You don't make any money writing talented stuff, Helen," Laura reminded me, "anyway I failed my English A Level."

"Did you shift James?" Daisy asked when I eventually escaped from the mobile and the literary madness in it. Sarah had gone to Girls' Brigade so Daisy was sewing at Mummy's wedding dress on the kitchen table. She is altering it into a size 16, with the aid of a series of photographs. Just in case herself and Johnboy get married quickly. Daisy is a bit concerned that the extra A-line panels in the dress could make her appear to be with child. Johnboy says Chance Would Be A Fine Thing.

I fed Bunty my shepherd's pie because I wasn't sure if I could keep it down and it seemed a pity to waste it when Bunty, who is now an adolescent dog, is hungry all the time.

"I didn't have to shift him," I told her, "fortunately the male to female ratio in Clublands didn't render it necessary."

It was me who took all those photographs of wedding dresses. For one solid week in January Daisy and I infiltrated every bridal shop in Northern Ireland. Daisy told the shop girls I was a journalist with *Vogue*, commissioned to write an article on *Northern Ireland Bridal Fashions For The Bigger Bride*. Then she tried on every size 16 wedding dress in the shop and I photographed her doing it.

At her leisure she is deciding what flattering alterations to make to Mummy's.

I told her about *Confessions of a Chicken Farmer*. "Willie thinks *Chain Reaction* had untapped potential," I said but Daisy had begun to sing to herself and couldn't hear me.

"Helen, do you remember anything about wheel slip in tractors?"

Feeling excluded, with my shelf-life running out and nothing on the television to take my mind off it, I decided to unearth a copy of *Chain Reaction* and read some "untapped potential" prose.

"I might even become a novelist again tonight," I told Daisy's unresponsive back, "and eat my nails and chain smoke and have a drink problem and be pretentious and whinging. Until it's time to go to Crete anyway."

"Well, of course Johnboy and I will not be able to go to Crete," Daisy frowned at me sternly, "we might have to get married at any minute."

While I searched the house for *Chain Reaction* I thought about being a novelist. Maybe, God forgive me, I needed to have another brain haemorrhage to fire me with inspiration. How could I get started again? Why was the first sentence always the hardest to write? What had possessed me to burn the sequel to *Chain Reaction*? What a pompous and stupid thing to do. I must have been pre-menstrual that day.

Daisy, ever respectful that creative genesis needs nurturing in its embryonic phase, didn't speak.

There wasn't a copy to be found. I became rabid and vociferous after searching all the bookcases, all the cupboards, down the back of all the sofas. Not a damned copy anywhere.

"Hold fire and don't get your knickers in a twist until Sarah comes home from Girls' Brigade," Daisy suggested, "I'd help you look but I want to get this sewn before Sarah comes home and starts saying nasty things to me. She said I was wasting myself on Johnboy the last day. But she might have seen a book during a cleaning fit."

Sarah was not at her most approachable when she returned from GB. Though she and Sandra don't speak, she had still heard that Sandra was pregnant. And she wasn't a bit pleased about it. Sandra, it appears, retards women's progress as severely as Daisy. Sandra was planning to spend the next nine months on her back. Who was going to run the Girls' Brigade? Who was going to teach Sunday School? Who was going to sing with Ian in his Gospel Group?

"Sarah, you wouldn't have seen a copy of *Chain Reaction* lying around anywhere would you?"

"What, your novel? It's probably lying where you last threw it at your ass."

Next day James and I did a pilot run with our survey. I wore flowery leggings and loads of lipstick so the farmers would think I was only his girlfriend come to give him a bit of company. And they would feed me with cups of tea while he asked the questions.

But, after endless driving because neither of us have a sense of direction, the first farmer chased us, the second was dead and the third was a full-time plumber. I started to think there was no such thing as a part-time farmer.

"Let's go and have a drink somewhere," I suggested, "and make one up."

"Oh we can't do that," said James, shocked, "it's against the rules."

So we compromised and drove on to Derryrose and asked

Daisy the questions instead. Daisy wasn't part-time but asking her about part of the farm would be the same thing.

"It will only take twenty minutes," we persuaded her, "and all the answers are completely confidential."

"I'm very busy," said Daisy, who was in the midst of domestic crises, "there were multiple births in the labour ward this morning and lots of babies kidnapped."

"What hospital did this happen in?" James asked politely.

Bunty was eating some afterbirth in the lambing shed.

"Would you ever stick your hand in and do the necessary, James?" This is a very great honour at Derryrose, to be asked to lamb a ewe. The last time I did it I left Gran Gran's wedding ring inside a uterus.

"I got carried away baking this morning," Daisy chatted as she grabbed her patient and coped her over on her ear, "for Johnboy's birthday. I thought I would bake an engagement cake in case he proposes to me. And I made marshmallow buns and chocolate rice crispie buns in case he doesn't."

I watched James from the corner of my eye. He was waiting at the ewe's bum for something to happen. In fairness he did not know the front of a ewe from the back. I decided it would be wise to change out of the girlie get-up and put on a wax coat and wellies or we would never get one survey answered. As I had no more rings to lose I stuck my hand in and operated.

"Baa baa black sheep, have you any wool?" asked James. James thought you grew sheep for wool.

"But how could you not know," I asked in the car, "one end of a sheep from the other? Haven't you got a degree in Agriculture?"

"Yes, but not in farming," said James.

"Well," I said, with a great big sigh, "you'd better start wearing the flowery leggings and the lipstick then and I will ask the questions."

"What a pretty boy," said Daisy encouragingly that evening, "real men eat quiche, Sarah says. They don't smell of BO and last night's beer anymore."

"You should have invited him in today if you were intent on matchmaking," I argued, "and laced the marshmallow buns with tranquillisers and we could have had our wicked ways with him. Real men don't fight back."

I selected a sample and chewed it thoughtfully. As Daisy is the only baker in the family it is important to encourage her efforts. Last week she made rock buns from peanut butter and Johnboy and Sarah and I had to eat every one of them because Bunty prefers afterbirth. We are afraid that if we stop eating she will stop baking and we will be back on the custard creams from Wellworths again.

"What star sign is Johnboy, Daisy?"

I had ridden Gypsy over to the mobile home that morning, and got myself both Willie's copy of *Chain Reaction* and the *Zodiac Guide to Love and Sex*. In fact, the book Willie had been reading was Derryrose's only copy of *Chain Reaction*. When Laura was pinned by the throat to the wall of the mobile she confessed that Yes, perhaps it had got mixed up in her departure luggage from Derryrose.

"He is an Aquarius," said Daisy, "why?"

"It says here in the *Zodiac Guide to Love and Sex* that Aquarians are unpredictable in love and often keep their loved one guessing. Have you guessed yet whether or not he will propose on his birthday?"

"I suppose that will depend on how good the engagement cake tastes," said Daisy.

In other worlds, and with other families, the engagement comes before the cake. But not at Derryrose. We are famous for doing things arse about face.

"Funny," I said consulting the *Zodiac Guide* for Daisy's star sign, "it says nothing here about Virgos having match-making tendencies."

"No," said Daisy, "but they like cake."

CHAPTER SIXTEEN

After two days of surveying we had two surveys answered. We got them both on the first morning. A sweet old man shepherded us into his kitchen and apologised profusely for the state of it – things hadn't been the same since "dear Maggie" died. What could I do but clean it for him, and smoke the cigarettes he forced on me for payment. Even if I had to throw up afterwards because the combination of stewed tea and cigarette smoke made me nauseous.

"It was my Christian Duty," I yelled at James, crawling weakly through tall nettles to the car. James hadn't accompanied me into the bushes, preferring to talk me through it from the car.

It was perhaps unfortunate that the next part-time farmer we cornered was a primary school teacher teaching his class the Evils Of Smoking. While James asked the questions I read a P7 poem entitled *Ashtray Perfume*.

Eventually we realised where our mistake lay. Part-time farmers all work during the day.

"I think we should be paid overtime for conducting these surveys at night," James grumbled on the first night operation.

"We won't get paid at all," I reminded him, "if we don't turn up with some of them filled in."

James was so like a child, but this was neither the time or place nor the person to try it on with. Bereft of maternal instinct,

I prefer to have a strong man to mother me. James and I were doomed to a passive relationship. But at least he had brought some salmon on brown bread and some sausages in his lunch box.

"I've got it," I said eventually, "your mother had a party and you are eating up the leftovers?"

"No, my mother was at a party and she threw all this into her handbag for me."

"Our first night victim," I informed him through a mouthful of salmon, "is a sinister old spinster who Mummy used to tell us was the witch in Hansel and Gretel. The one who fattened up little boys and ate them, James. There is a door from her cattle houses into her kitchen, and she has a pet pig called Lulu."

A bicycle lay sprawled by the cattle houses.

"Miss Devine!" I roared out the window of the Peugeot, "where are you, Miss Devine?" I didn't want to get out in case Lulu was a guard pig as well as a pet pig.

No Miss Devine. Her house had a mist hanging over it and one light gleaming ominously into the dark. James turned the Peugeot for a quick getaway.

"You go," said James, "you talk better to farmers."

"I don't want to go," I said, "I'll only get my feet dirty."

"Well I'm not getting out," said James firmly, "because I'm scared of the dark."

So, our collective nerves having failed, we drove back down the lane and decided to make her up.

I was very naughty to attend Johnboy's drinks party. I'm mitching off my six week Creative Writing Course at the Tech. Last week an intelligent girl read a poem about Socrates. Someone said, "That was just like a fruitcake," and I panicked and asked, "Who was Socrates?"

And a man who wrote twenty-six pages of foolscap about his "completely wrong" marriage was completely longwinded.

My right leg shook like mad when I read out *The Prawn Cocktail Crisps Murder* – the story of an actress who gasses her leading man after eating a packet of them. I'm going to wear flat shoes in future in case I break my ankle. I was so inspired writing *The Prawn Cocktail Crisps Murder* that there were bits of it on the back of my hand and stray sentences scribbled on hymn book pages. I had so many ideas I could be choosy.

"More drink," yelled Johnboy jovially. Daisy gave him a boiler suit as a birthday present. And six books of wallpaper patterns to choose kitchen colours for Derryrose. It's a test to see if they have compatible interior decor tastes.

James began to wriggle nervously.

"It's OK," I whispered, "he'll probably fall asleep in a minute. He always does when he drinks Jack Daniels."

"Did you know," Johnboy pronounced, "that it's the tradition in our family that the birthday boy sleeps with every woman in the room?"

"Ah James," I protested when he skipped to fizzy orange, "don't be like that. I want you to sleep in Derryrose with Sarah and Daisy and me. Three willing women, James, aren't you tempted?"

James began to whine about legal alcohol limits and the drink driving statistics in Northern Ireland.

I pointed to Willie who was pumping out *Paradise City* on the Karaoke. "With a minor degree of arm twisting Mr AC/DC will drive us home. He's not drunk, James, honest, he sings in tune when he is."

I added loudly and confidently that Johnboy's sister could take us home, she would consider it her Christian Duty. That was only bluff. Holy Ian would shoot us off the premises if we went scrounging a lift. Holy Ian would have let the lions eat Daniel in the Old Testament. And in her delicate condition the doorbell going after ten at night could give Sandra a hot flush.

"Well, I don't care," said James, defiantly, "I would prefer to drink orange and feel safe."

"Yes," I sighed, "I suppose you would."

"Look, Daisy darling," said Johnboy as we queued to give him birthday kisses, "thanks for the offer but you know I'm a bachelor boy. If we had to break the engagement off, would you give me back my ring?"

When Willie and I were jiving between the tables he informed me that there were two types of women in the world. The ones who tidy the house before asking their boyfriend to marry them and the ones who dance in pubs.

We were out of luck that night anyway. The police banged on the door and told us all to get home immediately. Daisy shook Laura awake – she was stretched out under a table – and we stumbled out into Ballyroan Main Street.

"Where is my hair," Laura screeched, "I've left my hair behind in the pub," and she started crawling around on the Main Street looking for it.

"I don't know what your problem is, James," I whispered, suddenly irritated because he had started to cry, "if you ask them nicely they will give you burgundy arrows on your prison clothes. Fizzy orange will not fail the breathalyser test."

"But I can't take eight people home in Mummy's Peugeot," he sobbed pointing to the police Landrover with a shaking finger, "we will get booked for overcrowding."

Willie must have thought the same. He ducked out of the doorway of Grubb's Pub and ran across the street to the Land-Rover. Then he came galloping back.

Wonderful, masterful Willie. "Johnboy and Daisy, grab Laura and bail her into the Mark 2," he commanded, "James, wipe your tears and take the rest of them."

"What did you say to the policeman?" I asked him as we loaded into the getaway cars. "Do you know him?"

"My mother used to go with him. They lived in a flat in Castledawson together until Colin was born. I just asked him what were the chances of pulling a car out of here and he said it was all right."

I looked at James shrinking beside me in the driver's seat.

"What's the matter?" James asked.

"Nothing's the matter," I said.

What an excellent house-party, we all agreed afterwards. Even the salted peanuts left over from Mummy's Christmas housewarming were eaten up; and the engagement-cake-that-wasn't; and the vodka-jelly Daisy made in a saucepan. After eating it James had declared that Sarah was his Behind The Bike Sheds fantasy at school. Sarah has been doing her Martyr Act since the confession.

"Don't you realise," I teased, "that James drank himself incontinent at a rugby disco once, driven mad by your beauty, Sarah?"

Sarah always becomes defensive when we talk about boys. "How many times do I have to tell you that I am not interested in men who judge women only by their appearance, Helen."

"But James grew up thinking you were sexy, Sarah. You should be flattered."

"Must I remind you," said Sarah crossly, "that 'the willie' has a mind of its own. The heroes of myths and legends were driven by frustration to conquer new worlds, raping and pillaging all in front of them. And then they blamed the beautiful women back home for driving them to it."

"I think we are safe enough with James," I laughed, "the only thing he could tell me about his holiday in America last summer was that the mosquitoes ate him at Niagara Falls."

"Well, maybe it's not a very memorable place," said Daisy defensively. James had eaten her vodka-jelly, Daisy would not fail him on a Traveller's Technicality. "All Laura remembers was that they charged her as an Under Twelve on the cable car."

"Laura is a Philistine," said Sarah firmly, "she is like that joke about the Americans in Rome. They said 'Rome? Was that the place we saw the yellow dog?'."

You see our problem with Sarah? The last time she laughed was when Daisy fell on her bum at the ice rink.

Sarah continued, "The only culture Laura brought back from America was her Calvin Klein jeans."

"That's not fair," I said, "she brought The Yank for herself, a recipe for ice-cream cake for Daisy, and a bottle of Yukon Jack for me. Lee used to make us a cocktail thing called Husky Piss and recite a poem and we would knock it back. Something about 'Beware the yellow snow where the huskies go.' I always meant to write it down. Laura says she only remembers it when she's drunk. That's real American Culture, Sarah."

But Sarah can think of nothing but Crete. She says Crete is a land flowing with olive oil and honey. We will look up and Helios will be riding his sun chariot across the sky, we will look down and the three-headed dog will be guarding the gates of Hell.

"In fact," said Sarah pompously, "the only dark cloud on my Aegean horizon is my travelling companions. Willie Simpson cornered me last night in the kitchen to tell me he and Laura had been 'At It' before they came out."

"At what?" I asked, "surely they have got past the squeaky bed stage by now."

"Farting actually. Willie doesn't break wind like civilised people. His are SBD – Silent But Deadly."

"Well, if Laura didn't mind," I said reasonably, "why should you?"

"Oh, you are so bohemian, aren't you, Helen?" Sarah told me sarcastically. I am hoping we will get lost in the Labyrinth and the Minotaur will eat Sarah. And then Eros will strike me with his love arrows.

CHAPTER SEVENTEEN

Laura and Willie arrived with a carryout of Diamond White to find Bunty prostrate on the back of the sofa, her forelegs round my neck giving me great big doggy kisses.

"It's research for my latest story," I explained, "for the Creative Writing Class – I'm calling it *The Dog with the Suffocating Eyes.*"

Laura laughed, snatching at the page I was writing on.

"Jesus, Helen, your handwriting is still dyslexic. I can't make out a word of this."

"No chance of you copying it then." I handed the page to Willie for approval. Willie won't come to the workshops with me – he can't work with amateurs, he says.

As an adolescent, illegible handwriting was the only means of protecting my diary secrets from Laura. Laura never had enough imagination to write her own diary but was skilled with a Kirbigrip to pick the lock on mine.

"We don't have to copy you," Willie announced proudly taking off his biker jacket and boots to reveal the Writing Pyjamas, "Laura has opened a whole new avenue of creative thought. Take it away, Laura."

Laura pulled some foolscap from her Wellworths bag and read:

" 'I gave you that large glass of water so you will have to run to the toilet all night, ha ha ha – have you drunk any of it? I'd like to think

that if I brought you it you would drink it. Let me have a sneak read, Laura. Why won't you? I bet you are writing something bad about me. You always run me down to Hell. Makes me wonder if I'm the man you want to be with.

I haven't used my new Sellotape dispenser yet. Willie Simpson and his Sellotape dispenser. 'Will I stick the curtains to the wall with it?'

We are nearly out of Orange Quosh, Laura – will we last to the weekend?

Did you see my mother laughing when you said 'prostitute'? I think she has a wee want. I wasn't refusing to have sex with you, pet. It was a small misunderstanding on your part as usual.

Laura, you are hounding me. I am being hounded by the press. Have you no inspiration of your own, that you have to be so sneaky? You want a bit of humpty dumpty, I refuse, you drop the book on my toe and then you write down everything that I blabber.

Will you buy marmalade when you do the shopping next? I like a little bit of marmalade.

You are taking advantage of me, Laura, your poor chicken farmer lover. I noticed Slack Alice was really into the wine. I offered it to her expecting her to refuse but she knocked it back. How dare you say that about my mother. My mother is a gentleman.

We have nearly eaten all the food from last week. One step closer to your diet, fattie.

I can feel myself sweating already – let's throw all the blankets off the bed – you weren't so ho ho ho earlier more like huff huff huff. Ah come on, Laura, pull off the blankets before I stick to the sheets. We can hug closer'."

Willie was beaming, "Isn't she marvellous? It's a completely new departure in creative writing. I lie in bed and chat and Laura writes it all down. Tonight it's my turn to do the writing.

And tomorrow we are going to the Stock Car Races and Laura is going to record everything the commentator says."

I laughed, "I particularly like the bit about your mother being a gentleman, Willie. Makes *The Dog with the Suffocating Eyes* a very amateur effort in comparison."

"It's not a novel anymore," Laura corrected, picking up *Memoirs of Field Marshal Bernard Montgomery* that Bunty was lying on. We were At War, even Sarah was permitting 24 hour coverage of the Gulf thing, but I was finding it hard to believe that the Field Marshal carried *Pilgrim's Progress* and the Bible into battle with him. I would have brought a German phrase book.

"The novel got boring," Laura explained, "and after Burgundy Balls's confession last night we thought a series of monologues would be better crack."

"Tell me," she added casually, "would you have married Bloody Richard if he had asked you?"

"The subject of Richard Knight and myself," I glanced at Willie, "gives me a pain, like indigestion."

Laura was only teasing. She didn't want a truthful answer. How could I say Yes when

a. I didn't know

b. Even if I did know I wouldn't have told her.

"That's what is so maddeningly incomprehensible about you," Laura yelled, suddenly excited, "you evasive tart. You will be useless in our Monologue unless we do a section on people who can't answer a direct question."

Mummy's ears were fire-engine red when she burst in through the back door – I'm not one for gossip but she has been extolling the virtues of Concord wine for a week now.

Aunt Maisie married Bobby Lennox in Barbados. Clad in a

white handkerchief of a swimsuit, she had joined the production line of British Brides doing it in the Caribbean. The hotel had given them a basket of fruit in their room and a free manicure in bed. Aunt Maisie was spending those important first few days of married life coming to terms with the shock of being a Mrs. As Daddy says, at least she had the wit to marry the first white millionaire who had taken her. Aunt Maisie is a giddy old bird – she could just as easily have run away with the shoe-shine boy.

"Aunt Maisie tells me that 27% of women think they married the wrong man," said Mummy, "but who can they compare him with I want to know? I mean every time your father hung his trousers over the end of the bed I got pregnant, but I'm not complaining. Ruth Paisley, my 2.8-fuel-injected-Ford-Capri friend, left Johnny because he pulled the bedclothes off her. She used to wear a nightie with fur round the bottom to keep her ears warm. Then she took up with the nose-picking Sid. She says Sid makes her laugh and laughter is the greatest aphrodisiac but half the time I don't know if she's laughing with him or laughing at him."

"People rarely marry the love of their lives," I said, "wasn't Aunt Maisie very shrewd to marry for money when there was no chance of her marrying for love?"

"This is far too deep for me," said Laura. "Come to the stock car races with us tomorrow, Helen. I will need you to hold my hand when Willie is risking life and limb to impress me. I don't think The Yank was the wrong man for me. But I was the wrong woman for him."

"Are you driving then, Willie?" I asked him, "did you finally find the drive shaft of a Mark 2 Escort or whatever it was that you were looking for?"

"I did indeed. Number 69 is rearing to go. And Laura has promised to drive in the Ladies' Race if Johnboy or I haven't her writ off before it."

"But Laura, you can't drive a car."

We pulled out of Willie's yard just two hours later than planned, number 69 travelling on a trailer, it took us two hours to pull out of a hedge (69, so the number is the same whether the car is on its roof or not; 69, because Willie says it's his favourite position).

As we arrived, there was an announcement from the commentary box, situated on the top floor of a red double decker bus (there was a bar on the bottom floor):

"We need some help here. There are three casualties on the track." And Johnboy and Willie went pale and started saying things like, "You go first, I have a funny pain."

"Are you writing it all down?" I enquired of Laura who was standing guard at the door of an abandoned DOE teahouse which served as the Ladies' Loo.

"It's Willie's turn today. Stock car racers use very colourful language, Helen. You know, highbrows will call our series of monologues 'Social Anthropology' when they read them. Hurry up, Helen, I might be missing something."

"Don't you dare leave me," I threatened, "if only there was a door on this teahouse you could come in and join me. There are three bog holes cut in the ground. We could have a party."

We joined Willie and Johnboy in the bar.

"Oh God," said Johnboy of the last race, "I counted them going out and I counted them coming back. Seven went out and only two came back."

"You are watching too much Gulf War on the television," I said knowledgeably, "you and Willie go and change your tyres to Wets. After that skiff of rain the Mr Bean family beside us changed theirs."

With them gone Laura and I sheltered behind a placard board that said "Have A Break Have a Burger" to watch the Saloon Race.

"No bulldozing, boys," the commentator roared as a Fiat Uno, a Vauxhall Nova and a black Ford Escort XR3i with personalised number plates did a circuit of the track to warm up the tyres. The Fiat Uno hit the last bend, rolled completely over and there wasn't a straight panel nor a piece of glass left on the car.

"Number 56 has tumbled!" roared the commentator.

We watched mesmerised as the driver, a girl of about twelve, limped back to the start, put her spectacles on and resumed the race.

"'Jesus sir, she can handle her but hi," Laura muttered as she scribbled down the exact words of a man standing beside her.

Willie won his race on tactical driving. It was a close thing with the Bean family car but fortunately Mrs Bean had held up the race so long giving last minute instructions to Junior that he ran out of petrol before the end. The Beans have a family stockcar instead of a dog.

Willie kept well back to avoid being bulldozed, and came second only because the four cars ahead of him died out, crashed or tumbled. Laura, who was taking photographs to brighten up the pages of the monologue, was disgusted.

"You'd better do something more exciting," she warned a trembling Johnboy when his turn came.

I returned from the Burger Van scolding that the varied menu did not include tea, only ice-cream, in time to see Johnboy tumble Number 69 in a fashion that pleased even Laura's camera. Johnboy said it was as well his brain was made of sawdust or he might have hurt it.

Laura's only disappointment was that Number 69 was so badly smashed she couldn't have a go in the Ladies' Race.

"Look pet," said Willie to cheer her up, "I've won a trophy. I know it's only plastic and I won it by default but it's still a trophy."

So Laura photographed it to please him. And then discovered there was no film in the camera.

Chapter Eighteen

Shifting Richard the night before the wedding was delicious, and sinful, and the only way I knew of keeping sane when he married Elisabeth. I don't intend to moralise or burden myself with a guilty conscience.

"Here Helen, take this tablet," Laura, like an overripe pineapple in her yellow bathrobe, thrust a glass of water at me.

I swallowed obediently. It reminded me of that time years ago when I was afraid to fall asleep because of the ghost of the dead boy coming in through the window. Mummy, convinced I had a guilty conscience, tried to bully a confession from me, but when "God is watching, Helen" didn't work, she switched from spiritual to medical help. She came home from the town one day bearing sleeping tablets for me. I was quite a big girl, and a better sleeper before she confessed they were TicTac sweeties she had been dosing me with.

"OK Laura, it's swallowed. What was it?"

"Valium," said Laura cheerfully, "I was going to feed it to you ground up in your breakfast, but you eat so little it would hardly have been worth my while. God only knows what you might say when the Reverend asks if there is any reason why they shouldn't get married. You will either mope and make the rest of us miserable looking at you, or you will get drunk and make an exhibition of yourself."

I smiled, and stretched luxuriously, thinking of the night before.

"There is no reason I can think of that they shouldn't get married," I assured her. "Don't they deserve each other?"

"Do you think Jennifer minds that Charlie is doing best man?" Laura roared from the bathroom where she was washing her hair and her armpits, "if he really did go to Paris with the bride that time to satisfy his curiosity?"

"Keep your voice down, Laura," I snapped neurotically, "if Jennifer ever suspected that you knew, she'd never tell me another secret again."

"I do know," Jennifer stuck her head round the bedroom door, "but if my husband is smiling it's whiskey and sex, not Elisabeth that's doing it."

"Well, you know," I said coyly, "Charlie should have spent last night with Richard, holding his hand, comforting his pre-wedding nerves."

"Charlie was holding more than Richard's hand," Jennifer flounced into the bedroom, smirking, "and I'll tell you something else that will put the bride's nose out of joint."

"What?"

"Richard wasn't on his own either."

This wedding really has the most bizarre set-up. Though they live down the country Elisabeth's family are hosting it in Dublin. Jennifer says it's because Elisabeth is not half as posh as she pretends to be and Dublin is neutral territory for snobs. Not that it matters. They are still a whole pile grander than us.

So the bride spent last night in Mount Merrion and the rest of us were put up in Flowers Hotel down the road.

"Who was he with?" I know nothing about Valium, but the one I had swallowed appeared to be working.

"Some woman he has been doing a line with for years," Jennifer dismissed the question as of no consequence, "Charlie says Richard is so boring he won't even boast about her."

"Maybe she is married," I suggested.

"Like I said," Jennifer tipped the remains of last night's wine to her throat and knocked it back, "who cares? Oh, that was disgusting. Tasted dusty. Come on Laura, stop shaving yourself raw and come down to breakfast with me. After last night I'm mad for a couple of eggs. And get out of bed, Helen, you lazy tart, and come with us."

"Where were you last night, madam?" Laura pulled me back as we were going into the breakfast room, "playing musical beds?"

I pulled away from her. "Like Jennifer says," I said, "who cares?"

I put on the red sexy underwear bought with my first surveying pay-cheque, reconsidered, and wore nothing beneath my bridesmaid dress. Even if I did faint, as Laura prophesied, wouldn't the congregation be equally amused by nothing as by red?

I never felt so sick in my life. Sick and scared. Maybe I am allergic to Valium. I had prayed for rain, and God had obliged and it rained nasty, thin, unfriendly rain all day. The bride wore a huge fur-lined gold tapestry cape over "Bride of Frankenstein" in the church. Richard looked like a fairy beside her. If he hadn't married her I would have gone to pieces. Embarrassed myself forever. It was horrible. I could have stabbed myself and felt less pain.

On the outside I radiated calm and peace. I smiled naturally. I winked at Laura when Elisabeth yawned and looked at her watch in the middle of it. I nudged Laura when she sniggered at

"With my body I thee honour". Excesses of emotion are good for novelists, my head told me. In the future I shall be grateful for this opportunity to feel nervous anticipation and horrified dread.

When Richard kissed Elisabeth at the end of the service his eyes met mine. I looked away.

"What do you reckon you want from marriage, Helen?"

I have been to a lot of weddings in my day and the only thing that changes is the price of the food and drink. Daisy and I had agreed that today the lamb tasted strongly of mutton.

I shrugged. "Chemistry," I said vaguely, draining the champagne and hiding the glass behind a potted plant.

"Well, if I ever go again," said the bride who had hoisted her wedding dress over her head to negotiate the cubicle safely, "it will have to be love."

"That's boring," I said, "you already love Richard."

"Of course I don't." Carefully Elisabeth emerged from the cubicle. "God, these dresses are uncomfortable. The next time I shall wear shorts. Reminds me of the first time Richard and I met at a birthday party and I dropped the strap of my dungarees into the loo and he laughed."

"That's a lovely memory," I smiled, "and you are trying to tell me that you don't love him."

"I was only ten at the time," Elisabeth laughed too. She was being very friendly that day. She even put her arm around me.

"You really are my bestest girlfriend, Helen, and I'm still madly envious of your figure. When Richard and I get back from Tobago will you come down and stay with us for a while? I will be so bored after a month of undiluted husband. And to think, he wanted us to go to Kerry instead. What would we have done all day?"

"Stayed in bed?"

"God forbid. I wish I knew why he got his hair cut this morning. I don't even find him attractive with short hair."

"Maybe his mother attacked him with a pair of scissors. You know what mothers are like."

"He doesn't have a mother," she started to laugh again. "What have you been saying to him? That huge blonde on his father's arm isn't his mother. His mother died of a brain haemorrhage years ago."

"So Aunt Maisie has been sending us dirty postcards back from the Caribbean." Laura and Richard and the dreadful Fleur were small-talking together. Fleur's eyes roamed the ballroom, hunting more suitable prey.

"You looked decidedly green, dear," she told me, "too much champagne? Don't touch it myself. Frightfully common drink."

"Not enough champagne," I corrected her as she bounced off to chat up Richard's step-mother.

"Isn't she marvellous?" Richard winked, "real piece of the British Empire. Whole countries were run over by Fleur-types. Having tea parties, playing tennis, shooting the natives."

"Classifying and declassifying." I swallowed Laura's champagne in one vigorous, reckless gulp. It left an aftertaste like Andrews Liver Salts.

"Hi Helen, Richard and Elisabeth are going to Tobago. Isn't that where Great Aunt Maisie is holed up honeymooning with Bobby Lennox?"

"Yes, it's in some hotel that caters especially for honeymooners," I said, "maybe you'll meet them when you are there."

Laura slapped Richard's thigh intimately, "Maybe the four of you could have an orgy?"

Richard took his wife off to dance.

"How intriguing," Laura frowned, "they seem to be so happy."

"Why aren't you racing around shadowing them to get a dialogue for the book?" I asked her to change the subject. If Richard and Elisabeth could privately admit that they didn't love each other, yet publicly appear ecstatically happy – well, what was the world coming to? You could trust no one these days.

"Oh but I have been," Laura told me, smugly patting her ample bosom. "Do you know what this is?"

She pulled a Dictaphone from the cleavage of her dress.

"And I have been thinking all day that you were deformed, Laura."

"All in the line of duty," Laura smiled, "I have a pile of small talk here from the groom. Why did you think I was chatting to him? Medically, he's a fascinating subject."

"Don't be so mean," I scowled, "Richard isn't boring, Laura, honestly, he's really quite witty sometimes."

"I don't have to tell you what they say about well-laid women," Laura yawned, "Richard couldn't hold a conversation with a goldfish. He could talk about nothing but the microwave they got as a wedding present. He's going to have a microwave party when they get back from Tobago. We're invited. Scientifically it's too good an opportunity to miss. You could record the true feelings of the happy couple and I could back it up with their small talk. How did Elisabeth perform in the toilets?"

"Pretty interesting."

It's probably a jailable offence to seduce someone into your confidence, then publish what they tell you off the record. Then again, newspapers are doing it all the time.

"Write it down now," Laura bossed importantly, "while you've got the chance. I'll give you a special acknowledgement at the front of our book, Helen, for this."

She sat solidly in front of me, waving majestically at the dancers while I scribbled down what I could recall of Elisabeth's toilet confessions.

"Now," said Laura, when I had finished, "I need some cold truth from Richard. How are you going to divert him from his microwave and get him to open up to you?"

"He already has opened up," I told her defensively, "I did the Richard monologue last night."

"Brilliant!" Laura was impressed, "I don't care what you do with him, Helen, really I don't, provided it's in the line of duty."

It was unavoidable that Richard and I dance together but perhaps unfortunate that he chose a fox-trot which neither of us were any good at.

"Yourself and Elisabeth are a picture of happiness."

I small-talked relentlessly as we stumbled round the floor and he stood on my foot for a third time.

"And aren't Charlie and Jennifer well matched?" I added as we passed their table. The pair of them were lying full drunk beneath it.

"I think we have danced enough now," I stood half intentionally on his foot at the end of the record.

He looked at me quizzically, "About last night, Helen. All those things I said..."

I pulled away from him slightly. "What was it you said the

first time, Richard? About me being scheming and manipulating?"

I walked away from him bravely.

They drove away together conventionally at the end of the evening. Elisabeth threw her bouquet in my direction but Daisy was too quick and she caught it instead.

I cried all night. If Laura heard me she never mentioned it afterwards.

Chapter Nineteen

"Of course we saw them." Aunt Maisie sucked her cigarette and admired the whiteness of her face in a hand mirror. "Go and fetch me the scullery mirror, Helen, so I can admire myself properly. Isn't my skin marvellous for a woman of my age?"

"Did you talk to them?" I held a mirror at a modest distance from her old face, so she could admire its pallor and ignore the wrinkles. I was often tempted to remind her that every cigarette she smoked took five minutes off her life, but she might have given them up and lived forever.

She watched me wickedly, knowing she was playing with me. Aunt Maisie is an old witch.

"My dear Helen, we couldn't approach. They were touching and kissing and fondling. It almost tempted me to try the same with Bobby. They were all over each other. Disgusting," she shuddered voluptuously and I swallowed hard in case the dirty great lump in my throat made me vomit.

"You are keeping your chin up nicely, Helen," Aunt Maisie permitted herself a small smirk of approval. "Read a book, that will take your mind off it. They say the first three years of a broken heart are the worst. I find myself longing more and more for your grandfather the longer I remain married to Bobby."

Aunt Maisie when she was my age had decided to love my

grandfather, and had refused to love anyone else her whole life. She claims she uses the gullible Bobby as a toyboy to keep her ego buoyant. And to show off in front of us that she's not past it.

How cynical I am, but then I have just been dragged screaming through the most major tragedy of my life to date, so I can be excused.

"Was that wedding shotgun?" Aunt Maisie tired quickly of admiring her old face. "They looked so experienced together."

"I wouldn't think so." I turned on my heel to replace the mirror in the scullery before I broke it over her head.

"Well, I'm not a gambling woman," she shouted after me, "but I'm willing to bet tenpence there will be a baby on the way by now."

"Sexual intercourse does not automatically result in babies, Aunt Maisie," I told her stiffly.

"Of course it doesn't, darling. We had contraptions in our day too."

"Aunt Maisie is on old bitch," I informed Laura in a passion later. I don't bother pretending with Laura anymore. "She says Elisabeth and Richard were all over each other in Tobago."

Laura yawned, uninterested. "What can you expect? Elisabeth can charm her way into anybody's knickers. He'll probably be in love with her by the time they get home."

"Thanks, Laura."

"Oh don't be such a melodramatic bore, Helen. Have you packed yet? Willie and I have been co-ordinating our suitcases all afternoon. So we don't clash when we're out together."

We arranged to rendezvous at the mobile at ten, Sarah and me, to clean out Willie's drinks cabinet before our 5 a.m. departure. This is an Act of Mercy, not of Indulgence. Willie is afraid Colin, his ten-year-old delinquent brother, will raid the cabinet when he's away. When Willie was in the Costa Brava Colin used to joyride on the motorbike. He brought us Bunty back one night when she was rambling.

Mummy gave us her holiday advice before we left. She fantasises about the white slave trade, my mother. Last night she dreamt Sarah drowned on the thirteenth of May. Sarah promised to wear water-wings any time she goes near water, even a bath. Mummy warned me not to lose my head and jump in after Sarah. Find a big man and let him save her, Mummy says, but don't let him give her the kiss of life in case she catches something.

We were cruising at 37000 feet, at 590 mph, I was listening to the Pomp and Circumstance March No 1 on the in-flight entertainment and trying not to throw up. Sarah was complaining of cramp in her feet. Laura, still drunk from the night before, was whinging because I'd booked us in Non-Smoking and Willie was snoring with his mouth open. It was the breakfast on the plane which sickened me. Beans, sausage and an unidentifiable object that Willie said was soda bread but I thought myself had fish in it. The Hole in the Wall at the airport was Out Of Order and we didn't have £1.50 between us to buy me a Lucozade.

I held out till we were flying down the right side of Italy before I vomited. It was a magnificent example of Aerial Projection, the flight attendant congratulated me.

"That's some bird." Willie avoided Sarah's bared and lashing Women's Libber teeth to pinch the attendant's bum.

She was pretty magnificent herself the way she didn't drop her basin.

The Editor of *The Herald*, complete with six sons and one wife, was at Heraklion Airport. My life flashed before me as I crouched hiding behind a Greek litter bin. A front page spread of myself topless and badly burnt, and the headline "Sunbathing Burns Them Off."

Pure fantasy of course, because it was warmer in Antrim this morning. "Overcast with a stiff breeze," the pilot had described Crete weather.

"You're not puking again are you, Helen?" Willie, the only party member who smelt stronger than me, pulled me up to standing.

"No, freezing to death," I smiled at him bravely. "Would you be man enough to give me your jumper?"

The Herald family did not disembark at Hotel Popadopoulus, lucky them. Willie, stoical in his Proud To Be A Protestant T-shirt, rubbed his goose pimples and said, "The beer had better be good here."

Certainly there was a pool, and a pool-side bar and whatever else the brochure had promised. Pity they had not mentioned that the hotel was built on a motorway, and you couldn't have seen the sea with a telescope.

"They told us it was ten minutes to the beach through lemon groves and banana plantations," I grumbled in Reception, "they must have meant by helicopter."

No rooms had been prepared so Laura, defiantly optimistic, donned her new Primark bikini and, wrapped in a bath towel, waited by the pool for the sun to emerge. Willie, who hadn't eaten in nearly an hour, was yahooing at Constantine the Greek.

"A bit of all right, isn't he?" Sarah, cool and unrumpled in linen watched Constantine from behind dark glasses. "Objectively speaking he matches my identikit of the ideal man."

"He has hairy toes," I murmured as Constantine attempted

to explain in halting English that there was no food. Hotel Popadopoulus did not open until tomorrow.

"He can shave his toes," Sarah stood up, "excuse me while I gain an introduction."

"She's away to ask Constantine if he goes the whole way on a first date," I explained to Laura and Willie who were arguing over the last bit of airline shortbread.

But Laura and Willie weren't interested in Sarah's hormones. Willie's alcohol level had plummeted and he was displaying predictable symptoms.

"Stop sucking my toes," Laura shrieked, "go and make yourself useful and eavesdrop on Sarah's chat-up line."

Willie trotted off obediently and Laura explained that Sarah was the latest species for the *Chicken Farmer* dialogues. A whole chapter was to be devoted to the study of *The Frustrated Feminist On Holiday*.

Willie returned bearing Black Russians and the disturbing and unfortunate news that Constantine wasn't biting.

"Not that that has ever stopped a Gordon before," he suggested mysteriously.

Sarah returned wearing her huffed head and without explanation lifted Willie and dumped him, dealer boots and all, into the swimming pool, which was freezing. Sarah has been a faithful disciple of The Big Muscle Health Club in Magherafelt since it opened. Laura and I joined for a three week trial of exercise hell. The plan was that I would lift weights to develop a bust and she would lift weights to reduce it. I gave up after two sessions and transferred my deposit to the Turbo Tanner instead. It must have been in Sarah's hormones that she developed the strength of a Russian discus thrower and the body of a ballerina.

"Spy!" Sarah bawled as Willie dog-paddled feebly to a palm tree island in the middle of the pool. Tit for tat he pulled off his T-shirt to wring it out and yelled, "She was only asking him if she could have a room with a view!"

We had a great view from our balcony into Willie and Laura's bathroom. And they had a view into ours. So Laura could lie on her antiseptic flavoured sheets and wave to Sarah showering in water-wings across the way.

Willie, who was both foolish and daring, could leap between balconies. It confirms our suspicions that though we Gordons are related to God the Simpsons have evolved from the ape.

Willie only had the one pair of boots with him so he was handicapped somewhat wearing Laura's flip-flops when we sauntered into Malia that evening.

"You told me there would be lager louts and T-shirts hanging outside shops," he reminded Laura as we were ushered through a forest of pink flowers to a brightly painted table under paper lanterns. Greek music floated gently towards us on the breeze.

"You said, Laura," Willie protested as a tray of exquisite Greek grub was placed before us and Sarah thanked a Constantine-like waiter in exquisite Greek learned from a Teach Yourself Greek cassette she has been playing in the Metro since paying for her holiday.

"It's not that I want to buy a T-shirt or anything, Laura." Willie poked at his mushrooms in garlic and cream and asked the Constantine look-a-like why they didn't look like the mushrooms in garlic and cream you got in Magherafelt.

"Drink your beer like a good boy," Laura advised sweetly, "before I beat you round the head with a flip-flop."

It wasn't Willie's night. His minute steak was gone with one bite and he complained that he still felt hungry when I fed him all the fruit adorning my Gin Fizz. There were enough pieces of banana and apple decorating the frosted glass to keep him regular for a week.

And somewhat mollified by the free raki after dinner he stubbed his toe flip-flopping out of the restaurant. But bravely he continued to Heaven Disco on Sun Beach Road to pump up the volume with The Pub Crawl who were all dressed in white T-shirts so none of them got left behind. Finally in his element Willie forgot the toe and bounded off to dance with a blow-up doll while Sarah was whisked away by a Pub Crawler who asked her how she liked her eggs for breakfast.

"Unfertilised," said Sarah, chilling out from final surrender. We all agreed that unchained wantonness often took years instead of hours to acquire.

Willie was so busy with his doll he missed the free cocktails so he insisted on ice-cream before leaving Heaven. His ice-cream lasted three Jack Daniels and an unrecorded number of Black Russians. He hailed a taxi by falling out in front of it.

Back in Hotel Popadopoulus, in bed afterwards, with animal cries singing across the balcony I dreamed I was on a tropical island, Tobago perhaps. I lay in a hammock shaded from the tropical sun by palm trees fringing a sea of luminous turquoise green. I was happy.

I woke with my face wet with tears.

❧ Chapter Twenty ❧

How did Laura and Willie guess that the Free Drink at the Reps' Welcome Party was Lucozade, Dilute to Taste? "Meet the Reps for the Reps are Here, The Reps to Entertain You."

Sarah and I yahooed to them from the washroom window, but eventually breakfasted alone on cold coffee and hard cake which we wouldn't have fed to Daisy's pig at home, but as it was Greek coffee and Greek cake we agreed it was culture.

Mysteriously Hotel Popadopoulos had opened during the night. White English bodies sipped Lucozade self-consciously and entered the Free Draw for the Meze Night.

"Well, I don't care if it is an artificial tourist attraction," said Sarah, clad in psychedelic swimwear, lounging beneath a parasol, sheltering from driving rain, "I might never get the chance again to see Constantine in a frilly dress and tights."

She sounded like Daisy's interpretation of marriage.

Willie was pushing Laura into the pool and dive-bombing into the water after her. Madonna serenaded us from the poolside speakers. Constantine's limited English vocabulary extended to "Madonna, she very sexy." Sarah preened herself every time he appeared. I awaited the appearance of Mrs Constantine with interest.

Gregarious as ever, Willie tried through animal means to tempt us all into the pool, but I threw a chair at him – he understands that type of language. When he had swallowed half the water he bored of playing Drowning and suggested we stroll into town for bananas. Since last night's Gin Fizz supplement Willie has developed a crush on Greek bananas which he claims taste more like bananas than Irish bananas. Willie's banana obsession only confirms our suspicions of his Primate ancestry. Willie had other plans for Malia. In his hazy state last night he had collapsed over a board advertising Full English Breakfast. So while he made a Primate of himself Sarah and I drank Retsina wine and ate nuts that tasted like the sweepings from a toilet floor. But it was OK because they were the sweepings from a Greek toilet floor. At first I thought the wine was off, that my glass wasn't washed properly, that I had really been given Clean-O-Pine by mistake, but Sarah, who had been advised by Constantine before departure, assured me it was the Taste of Culture.

Willie fell in love with a Mini Moke, soon to be re-christened Mini Boke. Beep Beep. Forget the Reps' advice about Hertz – "You have tried the rest, now try the best, give it a test." Willie recognised stock car potential in his dodgem car reject the second he put his foot to the floor. We were off. The map blew from Laura's hand as we took the first corner on two wheels and headed in the direction of Kritsa.

Kritsa in the Mountains, Sarah informed us: a town known for its handicrafts, commanding a fine view of the Bay of Mirabello. Sarah ate the Travel Guide before she left Derryrose. We were going to buy Daisy bits of lace for her wedding dress in Kritsa. Then we were going to walk for forty-five minutes through the Greek countryside to Goulas and admire the fantastic view down to the sea. I was looking forward to that bit. I hadn't seen the sea since arriving.

Kritsa in the mountains. Picturesque with winding streets and lace hanging from every shop front, and the owners prostituting themselves for your attention. Look at a tablecloth twice and you were propelled in to look at the rest, a calculator was thrust upon you and the offer of twenty percent discount proposed.

Horribly discouraged, I realised there wasn't one piece of lace I could have bought for Daisy's wedding dress. Feeling uncomfortably homesick, I was suddenly glad of a glass of local wine that tasted reassuringly like Mummy's home-brew. Perhaps they have gooseberries in Crete too.

Willie and Laura returned bearing espadrilles for Willie who was delighted because he had beaten the shop assistant down to half price. Unlike me, he felt no twinge of conscience about bartering with the scrupulously honest if rather over-powering natives. I wasn't built for foreign adventure. I refused to join them in a tablecloth shop where Willie bartered for half an hour for one with embroidered strawberries, then ran away when the woman was wrapping it.

There they were, a quiet Greek family, harvesting a potato field the size of the swimming pool in Hotel Popadopoulus. Willie descended on them like Zeus from a clap of thunder. Sarah's Teach Yourself Greek tape did not cover such pleasantries as "Can I give you a hand?", "Let me drive the tractor" and "How about a bag of spuds as a Thank You present?" She strode ahead of me, shining with insect repellent, to the Goulas Viewpoint. I stumbled in her wake complaining about the state of my white Laura Ashley espadrilles that cost ten times the price of Willie's. I tried to photograph the view but Willie leapt in at the last minute and mooned right into my picture.

I spent the Scenic Route back to Malia wrapped round the roll bar of the Mini Boke, eyes tightly shut so I couldn't see the drop below me and vomit with fear.

"Don't bloody let go of those spuds," Willie roared taking his eyes off the road and steering Mini Boke towards eternity.

We stopped off in a tiny seaside village to order fried potatoes. The taverna owner, grumbling loudly, took a bucket to her outhouse, loaded it with spuds and took nearly an hour frying them. Sarah wouldn't eat because she said it was rude to eat at siesta time. Really she was saving herself for the Meze Night.

Back in Malia she eagerly suggested we drive the potatoes home and let Willie and Laura search for a blow-up beach toy themselves. Sarah wanted to cover herself in carrot juice and catch the rays.

"Constantine sees girls like you every fortnight," I cautioned her.

So while Sarah cornered Constantine by the postcard stand to ask him about Minoan Civilisations, Willie played Jaws with his blow-up alligator. Constantine was more impressed with Willie's alligator, and the way Laura's bikini top kept slipping off when she jumped into the swimming pool.

"Constantine says he had a banana plantation before he had a hotel," Sarah informed me breathlessly as I dabbed brown vinegar on my carrot skin that evening and she carefully changed under a towel. Sarah and I shared a bath when we were youngsters but no one has seen her secondary sexual characteristics since they developed.

"I know," I complained, "didn't you make me stand with you like a gooseberry?"

"All in the line of duty," she smiled indulgently, "soon he will be mine."

I did not approve of Operation Constantine. We Gordons are beautiful women, charming, intelligent, desirable. Legions of men have chased us. "'Fuck me,' said the Queen Bee and thousands died in the rush."

"I am not being swept away by lustful desires," she smothered herself in *Obsession*, "you should know by now that I don't make hasty judgements. Mentally I have been chalking up a Compare and Contrast of our needs, wishes and personalities."

"Have you also chalked up the fact that he can't speak English on your Personality Profile?"

She was fantasising loudly when I left her. Constantine would be in Reception when she descended. His body would be unforgettable in a frilly dress and tights. His hard brown muscular arms would reach for her. From a small, black, expensive box he would offer her a token of his devotion. And it would not be a packet of condoms either.

"So, Constantine, are you married?"

Slippy-tit that I am, I sneaked downstairs prematurely to check if Constantine's intentions could be honourable, even if Sarah's weren't. I didn't want Sarah making a pineapple upside-down cake of herself and the rest of our dolly holiday ruined. I had even brought the Greek phrase book with me in case he mistook "married" for "martini".

Constantine shrugged. "You are a very beautiful English girl, Helen," he said, but then Sarah made her entrance. Her heavy brown breasts swayed gently beneath Helen of Troy chiffon, she wore rings on her fingers and bells on her toes. Sarah, she very sexy. Naked she would have had more clothes on.

Constantine fell to his knees and kissed her sunburnt feet. How did Sarah know that the one night of her life she made a bimbo of herself it would work?

They communicated all evening, though they never spoke. I was weaned on sexual tension, I could sense it. The way they passed the banana in the relay race was a dead give-away.

"I haven't had a hot meal since I came," Willie complained, "I want to go to Heaven. Maybe the barman will give us free drink like in the Costa Brava."

I chaperoned Sarah at Hotel Popadopoulus. The dancing got more merry and Sarah washed her bare feet in the toilet bowl and splashed my face so I didn't fall asleep on her.

"If I gave you a tenner," she asked, "would you sleep on the balcony?"

The green hairs that sprouted by the postcard stand grew longer. The red English bodies looked like animal experiments at school, like the lamb Jennifer butchered to see what it looked like inside when she studied Veterinary.

Constantine produced his cousin for me. Spiros was about seventeen and had acne. I offered Sarah her tenner back again for a swap. Spiros and Constantine were going to take us to the archaeological excavations up the road in the morning. I was afraid to stand up to go to the loo in case I fell over. Sarah pressed her body really close to Constantine's as they danced but he held her decently. Spiros, who spoke better English than Willie, said it was because the family were watching. Constantine had his bananas to water in the morning.

Laura and Willie returned singing. Willie had won a bottle of raki for *Take Me Home Country Road* at the Karaoke in Heaven. Laura was going to practise *I Will Survive* all the next day and win another bottle. They had eaten ice-creams in a bar with a Union Jack flying. And this bar had half a roast chicken with barbecue sauce and chips on special offer. They were going upstairs now to drink the raki. Do not disturb.

"He will be mine, he will be mine," Sarah repeated getting into bed. Sarah believes in the Power of Positive Thinking. She believes that if you want something so badly you are willing to sacrifice anything to get it, then you will get it.

I kept her tenner.

Chapter Twenty-One

Laura and Willie said they would find a Full English Breakfast down the road and left directly next morning. Laura had sung *I Will Survive* so often she had a sore throat. They hope to find a deserted sandy cove and to frolic about naked and take sexy photographs of each other. They will get them developed in the One Hour Photo in Malia, not the chemist shop in Magherafelt. Willie once spilled silage additive over himself. He says the hospital took away the pain but left the swelling so he will photograph well.

Sarah changed her clothes three times. I said it wouldn't matter what she was wearing if she intended taking them off. She refused to wear suntan oil in case Constantine slid off her. I threatened to phone Daisy to tell her our frigid sister was making a pineapple tart of herself.

Sarah smirked. She said she had dreamed of Constantine last night. Certainly she woke with a smile on her face.

"What have you put in your eyes, Sarah, that makes them sparkle?" I asked her, throwing *Love In The Time of Cholera* at her and packing *Hollywood Husbands* into my bag. I was convinced it was the only sex I would get all day.

Daisy was preoccupied on the telephone. She had sent away for a Victorian style night-dress on special offer in *Woman's Monthly,* thinking it would be feminine and virginal for her wedding night. But the 100% cotton was so fine Johnboy would be able to see her body through the material. Daisy didn't know if this was a good thing or a bad thing.

Generous to a fault she offered Sarah her choice of the hotels already booked for her own wedding reception. Maybe herself and Johnboy could get a cheap honeymoon to Hotel Popadopoulus.

"Sarah doesn't believe in the institution of marriage," I scoffed, "it's against her Feminist principals."

"If you were in my class at school," Sarah smiled, "I would put you in the Naughty Corner, Helen. Tell Daisy I kiss her on the two eyes."

Spiros looked a lot older than last night, old enough to drive a moped anyway. Sarah, who usually nags about the dangers of motorbikes and how it's only mental cases who ride them, plastered herself invitingly over the seat of Constantine's big red bike and, hair streaming behind her, roared off towards the beach. By some unspoken agreement no one mentioned archaeological excavations all day.

Spiros had learned English in America, he said. He was a cousin of Harry Mark Petrakis, a famous Greek-American novelist. Rebelliously I opened *Hollywood Husbands* because I am a literary inverted snob.

"We are a vibrant passionate people," said Spiros.

"Are you trying to tell me my sister isn't good enough for Constantine because a couple of thousand years ago you beat up some Persians, and a Greek called Socrates got poisoned and another Greek called Odysseus got lost?" I gave Spiros the fingers, "I've read Harry Mark Petrakis too."

From my parasol I took photographs of Sarah playing in the

water with Constantine. My fair skin burns easily or I would have taken close-ups of her breasts to blackmail her.

"I suppose yourself and Constantine are real studs at this time of year?" I asked Spiros who was building a sand-castle.

"We are very desirable to English girls." Spiros dropped his bucket and spade to light up a Greek cigarette that smelled of camel dung.

The girls under the neighbouring parasol were the real ugly office types and talked endlessly about nail varnish, clothes and hair. Spiros liked the one with the fleshy well-fed bum. I was so bored I thought of digging a hole in the sand and dropping myself in it.

"Give us a go on your moped, Spiros," I jumped off the sunbed, "I'm going up to the Taverna to drink myself silly."

But then Willie and Laura returned in the Mini Boke full of beer and wise chat. A pair of wrinklies had seen them frolicking naked and thought it was a nudist beach and had stripped all their clothes off too. And Willie had got so steamed up taking naked pictures of Laura he had thrown off his spectacles and smashed them. So himself and Laura had gone to the Tourist Police in Hersonissos to claim the travel insurance.

"Go away," said the policeman, "I'm busy." They returned to find him checking his Lottery Card and his assistant watering the plants. Then he started nagging that English people lost everything. In a month of eighty losses, only four were not British. Willie had to forcefully restrain Laura who was heading for GBH on an officer of the law. Willie said he could just imagine her in a cell with water dripping on to her electric light bulb and him having to bring her food parcels. Laura calmed down enough to inform him that British Tourists were keeping him in a job. Then she had to spell "spectacles", "Crete" and "Hotel Popadopoulus" for Willie.

"What is your job, Willie?" asked Spiros, fascinated.

"I'm a novelist," said Willie, "Yeats couldn't spell either. I get up at five o'clock every morning and take a cold shower and jog naked round the garden to get me going. In fact," he added, "I feel another urge on me. Laura here is my beautiful counterpart. I dictate and she writes. Like Barbara Cartland."

He stood up and Laura dutifully took a pen and piece of paper from her Wellworths bag.

"I think standing up," Willie explained, "so did Hemingway and Virginia Woolf, Laura says."

"My cousin is a famous writer," said Spiros, so Willie forgot about standing – the sand was burning his feet – and sat down to ask Spiros intelligent questions about the price of fame and fortune. Willie is afraid that *Confessions of a Chicken Farmer* will make him so notorious no one will ever speak to him again.

"Sarah hasn't come out of the water all day," I complained to Laura, "and she hasn't worn her water-wings once. She's going to catch sunstroke."

Laura shrugged, "As long as that's all she catches."

Laura lent me her basque to go to the Karaoke. It was a nice red nylon thing covered in black lace that she got in Dorothy Perkins before we came to Crete, but as my cleavage doesn't hold up the front of it I had to stuff a pair of bikini bottoms into each cup. Sarah serenaded me loudly from the washroom. She plans to sing *Don't Go Breaking My Heart* at the Karaoke. I yelled at her to hurry up because I wanted to brush my teeth.

"Sarah," I said through the bathroom door, "you are suffering from a seething mass of hormones. It's a sexual chemistry reaction. If he was Irish you wouldn't look at him twice."

"So do Irish men."

"Sarah," I said, "you are being swept away by a sexual chemistry blindness. If he was Irish you wouldn't look at him twice."

Sarah emerged from the bathroom, her silk dressing gown slipping off her bare brown shoulder.

"Unlike you, Helen," she said, "I do not leap into bed with any man who wolf whistles at me. I know what I want and I know how to go about getting it. I have never worn that see-through dress before because I have never had reason to."

I shrugged and squirted the toothpaste viciously onto the toothbrush.

"Well, don't come crying to me then," I said, "I think you are making a big mistake."

"You are jealous," she said.

We ordered three cooked chicken in barbecue sauce and chips and one orange juice.

"When I'm married and boring I'll eat real meals," I promised Willie who was scolding, "if I was a big girl I wouldn't have the confidence to feel all woman."

Willie shrugged, "Buy yourself a bigger pair of trousers, Helen, and keep eating. Look at my Laura. She's all woman."

I drooped. "Willie, my purpose in life is to turn men into a seething mass of hormones when they see me."

"You are very sexy, Helen," Willie patted my hand patronisingly, "in an innocent sort of way. Like Twiggy. I just fancy Laura more."

There was one stallion at Heaven Karaoke. I couldn't take my eyes off him. Willie, with a hint of detectable jealously, said he had been there the night before and he thought he was Elvis. He sang *The Wonder Of You*. I hitched up my nylon bra top and fluttered my eyelashes seductively in his direction. He came and stood in front of me, square and solid on two feet, a Real Man. I became a seething mass of hormones.

"Take the bikini bottoms out of your bra top," he said, "and I'll buy you a drink."

"It might fall off."

"I'll catch it."

He took a roll of money from his cowboy boot.

Sexual chemistry. I always get it with black-eyed, black-hearted Elvis look-a-likes. It feels like a time bomb exploding. You get a taste for it and then you're addicted, and then nobody decent will touch you with a barge pole.

When I went to the loo all the pores of my face were magnified in the mirror.

"Helen, he is plying you with cocktails to have his wicked way with you." Laura nudged me.

"I'm going to drink coffee and Andrews Liver Salts," I giggled weakly, "but not together. I'll be fine."

"Helen, he's wearing a dog-chain," said Sarah.

"You're jealous," I said.

I fed him bananas from my cocktails and he sucked my fingers. He pulled me up to dance and I walked into a wall. We danced and my breasts bounced out of Laura's bra-top. He caught them and snogged me on the dance floor. I hadn't felt so desirable, so light, so pleasantly drunk in a long time.

He took off his fringed black leather jacket and there were muscles on him where Willie, a tight man by Derryrose standards, didn't have places. He was a cross between John Travolta and Sylvester Stallone. We sang *Islands In The Stream* together at the Karaoke. He told me I was a tease, but he meant it as a compliment.

I have a degree in Agriculture but I haven't an ounce of sense. When sexual chemistry strikes I might as well be sixteen and silly.

"Come home, you drunken scut." Laura took me kindly by the arm.

I was in the bathroom knocking things over. Threw a towel over the towel rail. It landed in the toilet. Undressed and laid all my clothes neatly on the floor. It was fun.

CHAPTER TWENTY-TWO

When I was at university I used to drink too much and wake too early. A guilty conscience working me. "Every time you do something naughty God cries," Mummy told us when we were small. After the Elvis incident I woke at six. I had only been in bed for two hours.

Beside me Sarah slept angelically, dreaming no doubt of Constantine and how she was going to keep him now she had caught him. Wasn't this fantastic country the place for such a fuss-pot to fall in love? She came well prepared, with a suntan and a beautiful figure and clothes barely covering it. I envied her lack of imagination. I was jealous.

I phoned Daisy from my bedside.

"Daisy," I said, "I've done something really stupid."

"Helen," said Daisy, "I've done something even worse. Johnboy asked me to marry him and I said 'No'."

Johnboy, Master of Impulsive Action, had got down on bended knee with a daisy between his teeth and proposed to Daisy in the milking parlour.

"Did you refuse him because the Victorian night-dress is see-through?"

"I panicked. It was such a tasteless proposal. He was invading my interpersonal space, Helen. He made me feel claustrophobic. He said he wanted a baby. Apparently 84% of men aged thirty say that having a baby and pushing buggies is the most important thing in the world to them."

"How complicated," I sympathised, secretly wanting to laugh.

"Helen, I'm far too fat to be a bride. Mummy took some photographs of the wedding dress now it's finished and I look awful."

"Your personality would compensate for being size 16, Daisy."

"Johnboy is a thicko, Helen."

"There is nothing I can do about that, Daisy. Concentrate on his great personality."

"Oh Helen," she was wailing, "people only talk about personality when a person has nothing else going for them. Look how talented you are and you are moody as Hell. Nobody cares what your personality is. I want to be married. I had my eye on four Laura Ashley bridesmaid dresses. You can't go far wrong with Laura Ashley, Sandra says. I suppose you think she has no personality. Johnboy has started calling her Sandra the Sow because she has got so fat with the baby. Johnboy says it will probably be a boy because Slack Alice read it in the teacups and boy babies make their mothers fat at the back not on the tummy. Johnboy says Real Men produce daughters. Do you think that is why Daddy made five girls?"

"What bit of motherhood are you frightened of, Daisy?"

Daisy changed the subject. Daisy doesn't like to talk about the birds and the bees. That nastiness.

"Why did you phone, Helen?"

"I've made an Aphrodite of myself again, Daisy."

Even Sarah looks shell-shocked without make-up. Listlessly I sat on the toilet seat running shower water over my head watching her paint herself. The Feminist Commandment states, "Woman's chief aim in life is to glorify herself and to enjoy looking at herself in the mirror for ever more."

"Would you like some tablets, dear?" She rummaged around in her suitcase-sized washbag and threw them at me unsympathetically.

"I am not sick," I sighed, "I've got a guilty conscience."

"As long as it doesn't follow you around," said the charming Sarah, adjusting a straw hat on to her artificial head, "come along, Helen, Constantine is waiting."

I nearly died in the dining room. Elvis was eating his hard bread by the coffee machine. He waved at me when I came in.

"Go and sit out by the pool," Sarah bossed, "and I will fetch. What would you prefer this morning?"

"Ambrosia and nectar," I said, "or if Constantine has no 'God Food', a heavy loaf of rat poison will do nicely."

Sarah laughed loudly and humorously because she had read somewhere that men get really turned on by laughing women.

Curled up on a damp sun-lounger I resolved that last night's behaviour was character-building. I had survived worse. Elvis swaggered past me wearing his Islands In The Stream smile and little else but I concentrated on my yoghurt and honey. Laura and Willie tried to cheer me up.

"Come and drive the Mini Boke, Helen."

"Have some of my Coca Cola, Helen."

"You are browner than me, Helen."

Laura rubbed some Factor 4 into my shoulders. "You will probably burn in Hell after last night, Helen. There is no need to get sun-stroke now."

I resolved to stop drinking gin and start eating ice-cream. No hangovers. No guilt complex.

Sindy Doll Sarah was eyeing Constantine with villainous intent.

"Let's go over and tell Constantine that Sarah used to wear a padded bra until her breasts grew," said Laura, "and that we called her Frog when she was a baby because she was so ugly."

"I was a beautiful baby," said Willie, "I won Bonny Baby competitions."

"And tell him that her favourite television programme is *Little House On The Prairie.*"

"And she used to be madly in love with Adam Ant."

Sarah, noticing that Constantine was looking her direction, lowered her sunglasses seductively. "Adam Ant sat on my adolescent pedestal."

I sighed. I suppose Richard sits on my adolescent pedestal. As long as he stays on his pedestal everything will be all right.

"Daisy says Daddy slept at Derryrose last night," I said, "it's passive resistance to Mummy who has moved all the bedroom furniture in the brown and white bungalow so there is a wardrobe at his nose. He's used to lying in bed and looking out the window. He threw a wobbly in the middle of the night and tried to move the wardrobe in the dark and it fell on top of Mummy who was trying to stop him and they aren't living together any more. Soon she will be one of the 27% of women who think they married the wrong man."

Mummy had invited her colleagues out to see the brown and white bungalow. She had sat for two days on a deckchair in the rain supervising Daddy building ranch fencing round it. Daisy had been ordered to concoct fruit salad and rice and pasta dishes.

"It's not the other women," Mummy explained, "it's Aileen

Connor, the boss, I want to impress. I want her to think I work because I'm the idle rich, not because I need the money."

"If you splash the kitchen curtains you are dead," she screamed at Daisy who was doing the washing up.

She snatched at the towel Daddy was drying his hands with, "Stop using that towel, Kenneth, it's for the guests."

As Daddy says, it will be dark when the workforce arrive. They will not even see the ranch fencing.

"And better than that," I added to the sunbathers, "she has been crying poverty for months since the bungalow was built, and lying in bed at night worrying about the bills and the day before yesterday she went to Mallusk Car Auction and bought the most expensive car there. £7,200 for a blue Vauxhall Cavalier with a sun-roof, central locking and digital stereo. And Daddy is afraid to ask for £300 to change the Mark 2 Escort. Daisy says she is presently getting quotes for fully comprehensive insurance, with or without Daddy."

"Is she going to give the workforce a guided tour of the car as well?"

"She is going to drive them home in it. Daisy says she spent thirty pounds in the off-licence. The workforce are Catholics so they will be expecting free drink. Daisy sent her into town for a bottle of port and she came back out with Concord wine. She says God spoke to her. He said 'Jennifer, A Little Grape For The Stomach's Sake'."

Mummy and Daddy made up because Daddy had mixed and mingled so well with Aileen Connor and they spent the night in the marriage bed in Derryrose. Daisy has been counting. She reckons Mummy's menopause is so well advanced there should be no more little Gordons.

Then Daisy tried to wear Daddy's good body-warmer to

Castledawson Gymkhana and Daddy said, "Take that off, Daisy, I wear it in bed." Says a lot for Mummy.

Constantine was coming out with us that night. As I intended to remain sober for the rest of my life I promised Laura and Willie I would record all interactions of scientific interest.

"It can't be a sin to be twenty-four and to want it," I suggested to Sarah, "even if you are usually Above All That..."

"There is apprehension in your eyes, Helen." Sarah had refused to wear a sun hat all day and had burnt her face so badly the make-up kept melting and running off.

"Is it chemistry, Sarah?" I asked, "between yourself and Constantine or dolly holiday lust?"

"Both," said Sarah the Shameless Hussy, "but I also think it's because we are both so good natured and easy going."

There is no answer to that.

Having dined on something that was greasy, air-filled, fast-cooling and expensive we settled into Heaven. Willie dropped his trousers to reveal the sunburn round his boxers which I obligingly photographed for him. Constantine kissed Sarah's cheek a couple of times and held her hand. He had lovely, rough, man's hands I noticed critically. Richard Knight has always been the benchmark of male attractiveness to me, the way the Suffolk sheep are the benchmark of a lamb's carcass. Constantine graded seven out of ten.

I have raspberry ruffle ice-cream poisoning. I vomited all night and hardly slept, the pain in my tummy was so bad. Constantine left Sarah to our bedroom door and she slept through my seizure because she wouldn't know how to have a sleepless night if you paid her. At least I know it wasn't my brain haemorrhage back again – everything I brought up was raspberry ruffle coloured. Maybe God was telling me drink is a safer crutch to lean on.

I lay in bed most of the next day, crying occasionally with vexation and composing a magnificent story called *Smile Though Your Heart Is Breaking* about a stunning yet insecure woman who is so madly jealous of her blossoming sister she makes herself physically sick.

"What is the matter with me," moans the stunning yet insecure character, "men say I'm a tease and mean it as a compliment."

"How can you smile?" she asks the sister, who dies young of agonising cancer.

"Our Mummy told us to 'Smile though your heart is breaking'."

Chapter Twenty-Three

It was our last day. I prepared myself for a final roasting by the pool while Laura and Willie filled out the "What Did You Think Of Your Holiday?" questionnaire the Rep pushed under the door.

"Tell them ouzo is filthy stuff," I said, "and the bananas really taste of bananas."

"Tell them brown vinegar doesn't stop sunburn hurting," said Laura who had burnt herself so badly she slept wrapped in a vinegar-saturated bath towel.

"What did you think of the Rep?" Willie read.

Laura thought she was unapproachable because she had spent the last four days buried under Elvis, and not a love-bite to show for it. Willie thought she was superficial – she couldn't possibly fancy Elvis sober – she was only pretending.

But it was me, with no opinion of her, who had to deal with her when she knocked on the bedroom door. Willie shouted, "Come in if you're good-looking, stay out if you aren't" – and then he bolted and left me to explain why he didn't like her.

He was a rat deserting a sinking ship. He deserved another ducking – and his dealer boots had only dried out.

Meanwhile Sarah, Constantine and the Phrase Book took a bottle of wine to a secluded beach and Constantine told her that her hair was that peculiar light brown colour which merges into the golden, in fact such hair as the Middle Aged Italian painters associated with their conceptions of the Madonna. Spiros had done the translation.

Sarah tried her best to look tearful because she says repressed emotions cause physical illness. Clichéd even in a crisis, she informed Constantine that in life when the going gets rough he was to keep his eyes firmly on the bend in the road. On the bus she told me, in confidence, that Constantine and herself suffered animal magnetism for each other but their relationship was doomed because he wouldn't do as he was told. Sarah wants a Yes Man. But she is quite sure she will be too heart-sick to go to Sports Day at school on Wednesday.

Our flight was delayed two hours – Heraklion Airport was littered with crying babies and Belfastie children pulling each other through the dust in Dunne's Stores dresses. I sat cross-legged in a corner listening to *Scoundrel Days* on my Walkman and trying to write a story about being a refugee.

"We had a one hour delay in the Costa Brava," said Willie but nobody wanted to know.

"Ten ton polar bear," said a Toe-Poster type to Sarah. Sarah ignored him.

The Toe-Poster persisted, "You have just got to tell me your name because last night when I dreamed of you all I could call you was darling," and Sarah started to scream because she thinks she is having Constantine Withdrawal and The Toe-Poster's testosterone was making him behave like an ass.

Laura led her away to the Buffet Bar where the insolent Greek behind the counter mistook "Bottled Water" for "Buttered Croissant" and then wouldn't change it because the croissant was fingerprinted.

"Do you think I look like a writer?" I asked a Belfastie child who had one eye looking at me and one eye looking for me.

"You look like a secretary," she said, "or someone who puts on make-up."

Her mother, who was called Teresa, tripped over in high white shoes to chat to me. She and her husband were to come to Crete for a week on their second honeymoon, they hadn't really had a first one what with Natasha on the way and the shotgun being to her husband's head, but he had got his knees done. So she brought Natasha with her instead. Natasha had held a jumble sale of Teresa's old clothes to raise the money. Teresa had a party in the GAA Club and charged people into it. Teresa was going to write a Mills and Boon novel sometime when she got the time to do it.

I got out of the car and walked into the brown and white bungalow. "I'm home Mummy," I shouted and the first thing Mummy said was, "You have dirtied the carpet." Then she set down the Physics textbook she was reading and informed me that, "It rained heavily yesterday and the resultant surface tension has caused spherical drips from the laminar leaves of the trees." She is going to do a Physics O Level next.

Twinkle, the fattest and most spoilt cat in the world, smirked at me from his soft chair. Because Twinkle sits beside Mummy when she is gardening the little shite gets off with everything. Mummy has never confessed to Twinkle peeing or pooing or defacing her brown and white palace in any way.

I stayed long enough for her to tell me that Reverend Robinson had worn a silver tie on Sunday and she couldn't take him seriously anymore. He preached a sermon about working mothers being the root of all adolescent violence and Mummy says he has a poof's handshake and she thinks he is a bit of a Feminist. I think she means effeminate.

Daddy was allowed to drive the Vauxhall Cavalier home and

had hit it on the church pillar, scraping the paint on the passenger door. Mummy was so mad she locked him in the car with the central locking. They aren't speaking again. The last time I was at church Reverend Robinson preached about wives being submissive to their husbands.

I left my washing with Mummy and walked up through the garden to Derryrose. Johnboy was lying sleeping on the kitchen sofa and Daisy had considerately covered him with a blanket. She says Mummy gave her the What's The Matter With You talk and reminded her that at twenty-five she should be desperate for a man. Casual observation is only excusable at twenty.

So Daisy re-read the bit in *Lady Chatterley's Lover* about all the good fish in the sea and how most of them are herring and mackerel and if you aren't a herring or mackerel yourself there are very few good fish in the sea, then deliberated with her conscience.

Johnboy Jackson is a chauvinist pig, he asked her to wash his jumper and shouted at her when she shrank it.

He makes her laugh.

He infuriates her when he eats his nails.

He gives her a flash when their eyes meet.

She phoned Johnboy and he said, "Is that you, Lorraine?"

Daisy made the fastest (and only) decision in her life. Johnboy took her to the Radio One Roadshow in Portrush and got her drunk on Diamond White and ravished her in the sandhills and she decided that love was letting him eat her fingernails instead of his own.

They have been together ever since; screwing Eva's old kitchen units into our scullery, real untrendy Formica ones that will match the 1970's tiles; operating on Bunty's ingrown toenail; putting a sulphur and olive oil concoction on Gypsy's neck because they think she has equine sunburn.

Bunty is bandaged right up her left leg and getting so much attention she hardly noticed me home.

Johnboy and Daisy went to a Wedding Fayre on Sunday afternoon and got free vouchers for a portrait sitting from a famous photographer in Donegal.

Daisy spent half a day putting on face packs, setting her hair in rollers and painting her face with Sarah's cosmetics and when they were posing for the pictures the famous photographer had asked Johnboy if he was a model.

Then they started the Magherafelt Swim Challenge at the Leisure Centre, because Daisy still wants to lose weight before she gets married. They will spend the rest of the summer swimming 50,000 meters to get a gold medal each. It takes Daisy forty-seven minutes to swim fifty lengths of the pool. The first time she went the water was full of schoolchildren playing on a raft which they dropped on her head for fun. The raft was removed and they dive-bombed in on top of her instead. Now her Personal Best is eighty lengths. She says she had to go to the loo three times during it but she weighs two pounds lighter, the weight of a bag of sugar off her hips.

"Johnboy thinks we are stalling on the brink of the inevitable," Daisy told Mummy. (Johnboy hadn't actually used that language, Daisy says this is what he meant.)

So Mummy went straight to Belfast and bought herself a new hat for the wedding. Now she will save for the rest of the outfit.

Pity she can't fit into the Rabbit's designer wear. Sandra is selling off her Winter Wardrobe because she thinks when the baby is born, stretch marks and things will make her too matronly to fit into it. She sent a suitcase to Derryrose for first refusal. Sandra is always kind to people less fortunate than herself.

I have days when I wish I was more like the good bits of Sandra who believes God helps with exams, dieting and parking on double yellow lines. Not like Mick of the Shovel-Like Hands at University who used to go to Mass every day during his exams looking for Divine Intervention. Sandra realises that drinking and partying can't stop the fear of Hell and Damnation.

Sometimes I wish I was as plain as Mrs Reverend Robinson who Daddy says is a First Class Specimen of Womanhood. She wears American Tan tights to church and has a pageboy haircut and believes that when she prays someone on the other end is listening.

When I was young I prayed for fascinating looks that would turn men into seething masses of hormones. I would have done anything rather than be good.

So I fitted on the neat little suits in a frenzy of excitement. Daisy cooked a big feed for Sarah and me in the kitchen and ignored my dress fitting. But she came round at feeding time and, having scoffed two deep-fried Mozzarella cheese sandwiches and a new type of bun that tastes like Marathon bars with no nuts, she commented, "When I saw you fitting on those skimpy suits I swore I would never eat again."

I drank a glass of Cretan wine smuggled home on the plane and read my Stars for the coming month.

"The Love Planet Venus sways through the deepest desires part of your chart and can make a love wish happen especially with the letter K."

When Johnboy finally woke he took Daisy and Sarah out for a drink. Sarah is so proud of catching a holiday romance she is becoming a BFC (Back From Crete). Laura was a BFA when she came Back From America with The Yank.

I declined, preferring peace and quiet to drink the rest of the Cretan wine (the stuff that tasted like Clean-O-Pine). The Cretan sun hadn't made my breasts grow bigger. I'm not a fan of big breasts, I think they are common but two fried eggs isn't much fun either. I will have to return to Clublands and get Macho to hand rear them.

My latest story is about a Bad Boy, *Macho Man*. The one thing he looks for in a woman is her "arse". Women will do anything for him. Johnboy read the start of this epic before he went to the pub and says he should take lessons from *Macho Man* and jilt Daisy. Women never fall at Johnboy's feet.

Macho Man seduces a studious, bespectacled wallflower for some reason I haven't yet thought of. Perhaps he wanted to photocopy her lecture notes? He falls in love with her legible handwriting. The plot is that they both die of broken hearts.

I'm writing this because Elisabeth has invited me down to her newly-wedded bliss.

When I fell asleep I dreamed I was sitting at the kitchen table with Macho Man and he was stroking my calf with his foot.

Daisy says Johnboy took them to Grubb's pub where he told the locals that they had been watching the porn Lady Chatterley film before they came out. When Daisy told him to wash out his mouth with soap and water he reassured her that none of them knew who Lady Chatterley was.

CHAPTER TWENTY-FOUR

Sandra the Sow was wearing maternity stuff when I went to haggle about the suits. The Sow's wardrobe is not really the sort of thing I would buy if I had money. I feel rich and understated in Sandra's cast-offs, but secretly lust for glitzy clothes, maybe something in diamanté, or rhinestone studded. I think it was The Queen of the Rhinestone Cowboys who said she was reared plain and thought of the painted prostitutes on street corners as glamorous. The only prostitute we know in Magherafelt is Dr Hunt's mother and she is well past her prostituting days. Ruth Paisley, Mummy's friend, says Lorraine Scott, who Johnboy shifted at school, charges fifteen pounds a time. But she wears clothes that Oxfam would reject. I have always longed for *Pretty Woman*-style thigh high boots but as neither Sandra the Sow nor Oxfam can provide them for me I have to be content with tailored trouser suits and smock-like pinafores.

Sandra says that modern women fuss unnecessarily when they are pregnant. A woman's body is programmed to bear the fruit of her husband's loins. Sandra could jump over a gate or crawl under barbed wire if she had to. Maybe she won't bother going into hospital, but make a bed for herself in the stable and give birth Mary and Baby Jesus style.

"The natural way involves a lot of grunting and groaning and screaming your head off," I said, wondering if she was using her Bible as a maternity manual. Sandra was always impressionable. She used to go to Revival Missions, and Rock Gospel Concerts and The Good News Club and get periodically saved because the preacher had her convinced she was a backslider.

"Absolutely not," said Sandra, "Ian is going to lie beside me to comfort me during the birthing process."

"Whatever turns you on," I said, laughing, "but if the baby is coming bum first you might not be able to push it out, Sandra."

"Not 'it'," Sandra interrupted, "you will give my foetus an inferiority complex."

"In that case Junior may require a Caesarean," I instructed. "You can have an injection that paralyses you and they cut you open below the panty line so cosmetically you remain unblemished. Though of course you will never be the same down there again."

I know all the gory motherhood details because Laura bought the books. As with her English exams at school, I read them and told her what they said. It hardly mattered. Laura was so high on oxygen she can't remember the twins being born.

"I think he will be a minister," said Sandra, "I play him gospel music in the womb, and the sermon recordings taped for people in hospital."

I find this fascinating about Presbyterians. We are infamous for our Protestant Work Ethic – that hard work never killed anyone.

I know for a fact that when Reverend Robinson is not ministering to the demands of his congregation he plays computer games on his Nintendo.

Sandra says even halfwits can be hard workers, it takes a superior intellect and humility to be a minister.

If I ever have children I hope the girls will be beautiful. And if I have boys I'm going to feed them cow's milk, because in the past they used to believe it produced children with the temperamental nature of beasts.

"Daisy and Johnboy visited me last week," said Sandra from the floor where she was resting her back, "is Daisy still playing hard to get?"

"I know nothing," I answered, wearing my halfwit face. Mummy always warns us to be ambiguous with Sandra and tell her nothing. Good-living or not, Sandra can spread news faster round Derryrose than Indians can send smoke signals.

Sandra said, "Last week they thought they had finally come together. You know, sometimes Johnboy is in the mood and Daisy isn't and sometime Daisy is in the mood and Johnboy isn't. It's so immature when everyone knows that Daisy will make Johnboy a wonderful wife in the true sense of the meaning. Last Thursday they were both in the mood at the same time and I advised them to buy the ring immediately. And Mummy baked them an engagement cake and the ladies in the Women's Group are going to ice it with red roses."

Sandra might not have sold me her suits so cheap if I'd told her that Daisy threw a complete wobbly after the visit. Do Sandra and her mother not realise that the only people who will be organising Daisy's wedding to Johnboy will be Daisy and Johnboy themselves? Johnboy had to keep hugging her and telling her his mother was a lovely woman and she had to learn to love his sister.

Full of Earth Mother logic Sandra said, "Of course marriage is something that should last for ever and only be entered very seriously," as she got off the floor and fetched last Friday's

Belfast Telegraph. Sandra can't resist the odd dig at Laura who not only sins, but enjoys it.

"I've saved this for you, Helen," she said, "so you can look for a job."

Sandra the Sow Flemming, benefactor and patron of the Gordon Girls. She gives me pep-talks on the Presbyterian Work Ethos and sends Laura religious tracts in the post. I think there must be something psychologically wrong with Sandra that she is so satisfied with herself.

Sandra says the Bible says that every man (and I assume, woman) is born with a number of talents. Of course it doesn't tell you what they are, you have to waste the most of your life looking for them. Much the same principle as "You have to kiss a lot of frogs before you find your prince".

"Act well your part, Helen," she advises, "there all honour lies."

I don't know if she is quoting from the Bible or Shakespeare. I suppose it is one of Life's Great Tragedies that some people never find out what they are good at, or who they are good with...

In February I applied to be a Corncrake Fieldworker. As far as I was concerned the job would consist of sitting in sunny meadows writing stories while the sun beat down on my bikini-ed body and the odd corncrake hopped past en route to a mating ritual.

I went straight to the Magherafelt library and ordered books on bird watching and, while James drove me round the country surveying, I instructed him on the finer principles of migration and the RSPB. They sent me a PFO in March.

Sandra had helpfully highlighted the one suitable job for this week. Assistant to an Assistant at the newly opened three million pound European grant-aided Wild West Theme Park in Portrush.

She advises that I read *The Last of The Mohicans*, Sarah will brief me on *Little House On The Prairie* and I will watch all of Daddy's John Wayne movies.

I felt excited about the Assistant to an Assistant position. Perhaps I will be dressed like a cowgirl, or better still, a whore in a saloon bar. Fulfilment of my kinkiest fantasies.

So I reined in Moonlight at the brown and white bungalow and blew the dust off Daddy's book *The Pioneers* to take it home with me to Derryrose and study it for the interview.

"You aren't taking that book," said Mummy. If I had smuggled it out there wouldn't have been a word said, but Mummy was having a menopausal relapse that day.

"That book is part of a set, Helen, you won't bring it back."

"I'm only taking it to the top of the garden," I protested, but all protests were in vain.

Mummy has started the Swim Challenge. She swims with more splash than movement. It is ruining her hair and hurting her back, but you can tell my mother nothing. We all clubbed together and bought her a sports bag for her birthday and a card that said "To A Special Girl".

So I took off Moonlight's bridle and threw it in the hedge. There are many valuable perks to being Sandra the Sow's protégé – a "company car" and excellent references. Ian's father is a force to be reckoned with in fitted bathroom circles. I always ride Moonlight bareback – Sandra's saddle cost £600 and she expects it to be shining – so with such experience I'm well qualified to be Sitting Bull at the Wild West Theme Park.

Mummy came pussyfooting, "You can sit round the back with me, Helen, I allow you." I was stubbornly studying *The*

Pioneers in the front garden which doubles as a potato field and she was sunbathing in the sheltered back porch.

"Dictator," I said under my breath.

"I've made you a tin of spaghetti hoops, dear," said Mummy so I had to eat them to please her. When Mummy was properly menopausal she made us breakfast in bed every morning, all of us. Then as the day progressed and she suffered a couple of hot flushes and things, she would start throwing plates at us and the knives were always hidden.

"Are you still huffing?" she asked when I had the whole tin eaten.

"I don't listen to the ravings of neurotic women," I said stiffly. It was my own fault that she beat the head off me and told me I was ungrateful and never civil.

Sandra drove me to the Wild West Centre on Saturday. I wanted Daisy to come with us but she was getting a lift with Mummy to the swimming pool to swim sixty lengths and get her silver swimming medal. Then she will only have to swim another 1200 lengths to win the elusive gold. We have calculated that at twenty lengths a day three times a week it will take Mummy until Christmas to win her gold medal. By then we will have her certified.

Daisy says she hasn't time to think when she's swimming. She is too busy counting lengths in case she swims one too many and forgets to count it.

Sandra wouldn't come with me on the simulator Conestoga Wagon Train where you think you are being attacked by Red Indians. There's one at Portrush Amusements where you think you are on the back of a motorbike. Sandra says that everyone knows the Indians set fire to the wagons at night and stampeded the animals and stole them the next day. Sandra has been reading up on the Wild West too. Such a good and faithful servant will get a massive mansion on the Hill in Heaven.

There were no Saloon Girls in the Wild West Bar. Sandra ate a Geronimo burger and advised me on Interview Technique. You should always ask about holidays and wages, Sandra says, or interviewers think you are stupid.

"Junior is restless and hungry," she added as she tucked into her Campfire Fries. Presbyterians always eat up all the food they've paid for. By their clean plates shall you know them. Sandra is becoming distinctly sow-like. We stopped for a picnic on the way to Portrush and she ate two Mars Bar sandwiches, two pieces of fruitcake and three hard-boiled duck eggs. The one thing worse than a health food addict is a health food convert. Sandra is rejecting all E numbers in case she turns Junior into a hyperactive foetus.

I remember that when Sandra got married she asked for half a pound of liver the first day she went shopping and then asked the butcher should she boil it or fry it.

She claims to have weighed eight stones when she married Ian. Now, she proudly told me, she was two pounds under eleven. Sandra says fat girls are always the best looking.

It is a real status symbol in Derryrose to give birth to as heavy a baby as possible. I hope all my children are tiny and rat-like and pop out when I sneeze.

"So," said Sandra importantly, "the Job Description says you will be in charge of three Indians who skulk around the Park scalping visitors, The Lone Ranger who takes pony rides on Hey Ho Silver, a few Jacob sheep and a couple of spotty pigs you don't know the breed of."

I never liked pigs at college. Nothing personal but they made my hair smell.

"Can you acquire husbandry manuals for these animals?" asked Sandra importantly.

"Sandra," I said feeling frightened suddenly, "it is a supervisory and administrative post. I will never be near the animals."

Sandra wagged her finger at me. "You can never be too smart," she said.

CHAPTER TWENTY-FIVE

Mr and Mrs Richard JF Knight live in a Laura Ashley-fied cottage in what is probably the most picturesque corner of Ireland, bar Derryrose. Elisabeth says an interior designer did it when they were in Tobago, scenery and all. She sniggered when she said "our little nest".

Elisabeth met me in Dublin the day after I got the Wild West Theme Park job. My interview had been unexceptional – I plaited my hair and wore cowboy boots beneath a fringed skirt and they wanted to know why I hadn't boasted of *Chain Reaction* on the application form. Lowering my eyelashes modestly I suggested my talent for novel writing was hardly relevant to the position of Assistant to an Assistant, in an administrative and supervisory capacity. I did not tell them I was a Captain in the Girls' Brigade or a Stripper.

Sandra, who was acting as chauffeur, introduced me to her Aunt Ruby who lives on the Scenic Route. Aunt Ruby is mad for a Bed and Breakfast lodger who will take her up the 150 foot Big Wheel at the Theme Park. Aunt Ruby says her son Mervyn (his unfortunate name) is afraid of heights.

While Aunt Ruby was feeding us chocolate cake the Big Chief at the Wild West phoned with his congratulations. He thought I had the temperament to be the Assistant to an Assistant. But he wanted to know why I hadn't asked about holidays and pay in the interview. With a pay packet advertised at £13,000 I didn't feel it necessary.

I will share a bed with Mervyn, who is a Senior Lab Technician at Queen's University, Belfast and brings his dirty washing home to Mammy at the weekends. As Aunt Ruby and Sandra don't seem to think sharing sheets is unhygienic I didn't mention it. On my weekend visits from university flat-life Mummy used to make me shower before I was allowed into the Derryrose beds in case I had caught any diseases.

There are sketches of insect mouth-parts on Mervyn's bedroom walls. I impressed Aunt Ruby by pretending to recognise a locust. Aunt Ruby says Mervyn is writing a thesis on the Honey Bee.

If, for any unavoidable reason, Mervyn and I have to share the bed Aunt Ruby promises to put a pillow between us.

Sandra, thinking herself facetious, says Mervyn will be the only man I will share the bed with.

When I got home Sarah greeted me with, "Could you please ask in future when you want to wear my linen jacket. You have put make-up round the collar." At least she didn't notice the gravy stain round the buttons where I spilt my Chinese Chips and Gravy on the way home.

Sarah believes herself to be excusably heartbroken over Constantine. She refuses to eat and has been sleeping with Mummy. Feeling airy I stripped off the jacket and ate dinner in my brassiere.

I told Elisabeth I had never shared a bed with a Mervyn before. She has offered me a Richard any time. She says they have rowed steadily since the honeymoon so she has rented an apartment in Ballsbridge and might even work again.

When she told Richard, he was making a cup of tea and

dropped the kettle and scalded himself and kicked it round the Laura Ashley-fied kitchen a couple of times. They have not spoken since.

Elisabeth says Richard spent the weekends in Dublin with her when they were engaged. She thinks the weekends were enough with him.

We thought an excursion to the hairdresser's might liven up the drive to the cottage. Elisabeth wants to spend her dowry before Richard gets his hands on it. Elisabeth says marriage means what belongs to him belongs to her and what belongs to her she keeps.

Personal vanity and an inferiority complex make me the ultimate hairdressing victim. The inner voice that shouts "Fatty" at Daisy persuades me that if I only give the stylist a free hand I will be transfigured. Once I went to Magherafelt and asked for it shorter at the back and still long at the front. Simple instructions. When I emerged my neckline was shaved and an exaggerated widow's peak hung in my eyes. Mummy, trying to be helpful, cut the whole thing off and I wore her red wig that she bought to be Maureen O'Hara in *The Quiet Man* until it grew back. She and Daddy often act out bits of the film after church on Sunday. There has been many a door kicked in and bed banged to pieces in Derryrose.

"Your face is too thin for long hair, darling," the stylist said, "and isn't brown hair awfully boring?"

Famous last words. Hypnotised with hope that at last I would be beautiful (and Richard would become a seething mass of hormones when he saw me) I let the stylist have her wicked way.

"Trust me, darling," she said.

Elisabeth was taken to the back of the salon and vigorously

scolded for eating her split ends. Then she was artfully persuaded that black hair would complement her green eyes and the suntan she picked up in Tobago.

We met once at the washbasin. Elisabeth was helpless with laughter – she'd had black false fingernails fitted to match her black false hair and was considering getting her eyebrows dyed too.

"Richard says dyed hair and curly perms are sluttish," she was almost singing, "and we are having dinner with his Bank Account tomorrow night."

Which was just as well because it cost her £103 to look like a vampirette. With characteristic flamboyance she insisted on paying the £75 it took me to become Marilyn Monroe. But only if I bought a pair of really high shoes and walked in them with a wiggle.

"You know," I said in The Badger later when we were drinking ourselves silly on Happy Hour cocktails, "you could tell Richard the black is a home-brew on loan from Aunt Maisie. She dyes her hair with blackberries. Mummy always lies about the price of things in our house. She says it's the secret of a happy marriage."

"Certainly not," said Elisabeth, "and you have been paid handsomely to save my marriage, Helen. Richard and I will be eternally grateful."

Richard only gave himself away once. I was curled up in the heady and haphazard garden nursing a fragile head and wondering if Elisabeth would give me her cast-offs if I asked her and Richard walked straight past me in his wellies, did a classic double-take and said, "Helen?" in a bewildered, strangled voice. Then he remembered and turned and walked on into the kitchen. My heart was beating so violently I almost choked on it. The bad bitch hadn't told him I was coming.

I liked Richard's stepmother "Call Me Dolly" immediately. I liked that way she carried her fifteen stones with an elegance usually reserved for anorexics. I liked the way she talked about *The Archers* as if they lived up the road. I liked the way she kept Wilco, her potentially domineering husband, in check.

"Please Wilco, not that deathly boring hunting story again, darling. Helen doesn't want to know. You went through the gate the same as everyone else. Richard is the only person who ever cleared that ditch and that was only because he was trying to break his neck."

"So he wouldn't have to marry me," Elisabeth laughed. Richard hadn't commented on the hair or the nails. If I had been married to him I would have cried. In fact Richard had said absolutely nothing but "Pass the salt, please," since we had met.

But his foot sat obstinately on top of mine under the dinner table. He talked farming with his father and his foot said, "You are mine". I was getting a sexual chemistry reaction just thinking about it. If I never saw Richard again I would never stop wanting him.

"Of course," said Elisabeth, "my husband didn't want to marry me at all. He says he loves me the way you love a record or a recipe but he isn't in love with me, whatever that means."

Like an eavesdropper hearing no good of themselves I suddenly felt claustrophobic. The hole for my throat was closing over.

Elisabeth calmly kept eating her potatoes and said that being outrageously romantic by nature and eager to love, honour and obey her sweetheart she decided on Valentine's Day as the most appropriate, if rather unimaginative, marriage date.

"But Richard is so frightened of commitment he charged that

ditch with Kamikaze determination. Such dismay when the brown mare jumped it. Poor Richard. He can't even get his suicide right," said Elisabeth maliciously.

Richard's stepmother, Call Me Dolly, interrupted smoothly, "I am convinced wedding jitters are a genetic weakness. Ask one sufferer and he will have a dozen relations who have done the same. A stick of dynamite and a horse-whip provide the most effective cure."

"I suffer you see," confided Wilco the Bank Account, proudly. He was wearing a blue shirt with a white collar and a navy blue blazer, to pretend he was yachting, not husbanding. I don't know if Wilco idolises Call Me Dolly because she bullies him or because she holds the purse strings. "I suffered with both my wives. If it's hard to catch a good man, then by George it's harder to hold him."

Elisabeth ignored her parents-in-law.

"Richard sulked for a week because he hadn't the nerve to kill himself. And in the meantime developed a freakish behaviour pattern. He was in the bath one weekend and I went in to kiss him, an eternally romantic gesture one would think, and with a face that would have soured milk he said 'You will get soapy water in your mouth, Elisabeth'."

They say women often prepare the path of marital escape for years before they run away. Elisabeth says it only took Richard days. They went to the chip-shop the night of the soapy kiss and because Elisabeth didn't want to eat his chips he said, "Fine, you don't have to marry me either if you don't want to."

And he broke their engagement completely.

I felt very fragile as I listened. When we were young and wild Elisabeth said she hoped to be engaged many times, but never married. Daisy had been shocked when she said it.

"We were awfully civilised about the break-up," said Elisabeth comfortably, "there weren't any tears or anything. I even helped him carry his things from my flat in Dublin, the way you would if you loved someone but weren't in love with them."

And all the time she was scheming how to get him back. Elisabeth says she hasn't the temperament to be a jilted bride. It would cramp her style. She didn't want to be married to a man she loved obsessively. It was unhealthy. Richard thought so too. He just forgot sometimes.

"What did you do?" I asked with horrid fascination. Richard had stopped playing footsie with me.

"I bought him," said Elisabeth proudly. "All those deposits, the dresses, the photographer, the cake, the hotel. Perhaps I have Presbyterian ancestors, or maybe I slept in your bedroom too long with you at university, Helen."

She says she just put the wedding date back a month and kept on organising. She organised their little nest and got it Laura Ashley-fied. Richard didn't do a thing. He didn't dare.

Elisabeth says everyone has their price, and men are more easily bullied than women.

Poor weak Richard.

I used to quote, "Courage is not being fearless, courage is being afraid and going on."

Wilco had become bored with the conversation. No one was paying him any attention. He announced, "People try to live false lives. Sex is perfectly normal and should be acceptable in young couples. Of course they should live together before they marry. I approve entirely. I must say my wives wouldn't have taken me if they had lived with me first. A man has got to check she doesn't wear her underwear in bed, or have a teddy bear."

"And sex gets more wonderful as you get older," he added taking a grab at Call Me Dolly, "I have a secret technique. But I won't tell you what it is. You will only laugh at me."

Call Me Dolly lifted her eyes from her lemon meringue pie long enough to say, "He's no good at it, you know."

Chapter Twenty-Six

"That was the nicest porridge I've ever tasted, Helen," said Richard, "better than the wedding morning porridge in Flowers."

"Oh yes," said Elisabeth, "our wedding. I had such a thumping headache until it was consummated. The Management left champagne and strawberries in our room that momentous evening. The champagne was drunk, strawberry stalks were scattered over the room, Richard went into the bathroom to slip into something more comfortable. I put on my pyjamas and fell asleep."

Richard went to work (he did not kiss his wife) and Elisabeth shrugged. "All is fair in love and war," she said, so I didn't mention it.

But later, when Elisabeth was making a "dreary, dreary shopping list, how can marriage be romantic when you have to buy toilet rolls", I recorded the conversations in my diary for Laura's book, and wondered.

If Richard was cold and weak, why had I not seen it? I have known so many men intimately and pride myself on only choosing the finest specimens of manhood. Laura and Mummy say. "Take no passengers" about relationships. Maybe that is why Laura despises Richard. All these years, have I only been suffering sexual chemistry with him? Maybe it makes you blind.

I have been making excuses for him since I met him. I gave his parents a loveless marriage. I made his father a dirty lowdog, who seduced village girls and ate so much he had to throw up before each meal.

I made his mother silly and affected, a flibbertigibbet, a wife for show, not for motherhood. She would have resented Richard's birth, it would have ruined her figure.

I sent him to a cruel boarding school with prehistoric teachers. When he was a hobble-de-hoy, neither boy nor man, he never got the chance to become a seething mass of hormones at the sight of a pretty girl, like a normal adolescent.

He had never been allowed to express himself.

"Come in and have a piece of wedding cake," Elisabeth shouted from an upstairs window, "tradition decrees a tier should be kept until the first child arrives but Richard had mumps so we could be waiting for a while."

I had eaten a piece to please her when she remarked, somewhat vaguely, that she was never happy about leaving food in the cottage – "Mice, you know."

Then we laughed about the time we shared a flat and I was cooking in the kitchen and a mouse jumped out of the oven when I opened the door and I screamed and Elisabeth freaked in the other room and screamed and screamed because she thought it was a rapist in the kitchen not a mouse.

"Why did you marry Richard?" I asked bravely.

Elisabeth shrugged as she packed her shopping bag, "If you can't marry for love, then it's advisable to marry for money," she said. "Everything I said last night was true. I've been trying to get it off my chest for ages. So many women can't see past the wedding photographs, they haven't a notion what successful marriages are made of. Then the mist clears and they find themselves hitched to a husband with nasty habits. I know Richard's history – there hasn't been a lunatic, nor any severe inbreeding, nor a disease in the family for centuries. Apart from his mother's brain haemorrhage and they say that's not hereditary. We could fall in love yet."

"I wouldn't try too hard to fall in love," I advised, "my parents are in love and it's frightening. Daddy's chest was sore last week and he was an awful grumpy-head. So Mummy got bored with him and went off to visit Ruth Paisley and didn't come back until 2 am and when she got home Daddy had all the windows barred and the doors locked in the brown and white bungalow. He lay in bed and ignored her when she rapped on the windows. Finally she lost the head and yelled, 'If you don't open this bloody house, Kenneth, it's going up for sale tomorrow.' And Daddy opens the window and yells, 'Bugger off to where you came from,' but he let her in anyway. If he hadn't loved her he would have made her sleep in the garden shed. And it would have done her no harm."

Elisabeth laughed.

"Anyway," I added, "it is as well you are not in love. I don't have the psychological maturity to enjoy being the spare arm of a close fitting twosome."

"I was in love before," Elisabeth confessed suddenly, "maybe people only ever fall in love once? It was inexplicable and exciting and it actually happened to me. I thought about him constantly even when I wasn't thinking about him. But then it stopped and I married Richard."

To think we used to call Elisabeth "wide-eyed and legless" when we were at college.

"But you can't leave, Helen," said Richard, "not before your lunch. We were going to use the microwave."

He was just like anyone else. Willie Simpson thinks about his food constantly too. I zipped up Miss Havisham's carpet bag feeling faintly amused.

"Was it something I said?" asked Richard.

Pass the salt please, I thought, it had been the final straw. My air-castle had fallen over. I was going home to Mummy.

"Which way is Dublin?" I asked, "do I turn right or left at the end of the lane?"

"Elisabeth will be really cross with me," Richard pleaded.

When Mummy was small she claims she got a lift with Seamus Heaney's uncle. He forgot about her crouching in the back of the car and drove on past her house and in her panic she opened the back door of the car and leapt out. So of course in Derryrose, our impressionable backwater, Laura and I were convinced The Man In The Ten Gallon Hat would come back and kidnap us too.

We tried to practise the getaway move coming home from church. Daddy was taking the corner at King Street on two wheels racing home for his dinner – and Laura opened the back door and rolled out in her good Sunday-Go-To-Meeting coat. After Laura had been thrashed with a belt, the back doors of the Morris were sealed and it became a two-door car.

I was rescued by two cowboys wearing matching blue checked shirts and driving a Sierra Ghia with blankets across the seats either to conceal fingerprints or to keep the car clean. I wasn't sure about getting into the car with them. But I reckoned they were safe enough when I saw the little boy in the back seat. Not even Irish kidnappers would take their kid along.

Willie Simpson used to smuggle cars over the border and he always took Colin along as the "wee brother" decoy. When Colin was a baby he was trained to howl at the sight of a uniform, when he got older he was given sweeties to drop his trousers and say, "Daddy, I have got to do a wee-wee." He got chocolate if he performed on cue.

We used to do the same sort of thing with Bunty. Policemen were so busy ensuring Bunty didn't use them as a lamp-post that they never noticed the bald tyres and out of date tax disc on the Mark 2 Escort.

The "wee brother" was a hood. He walloped me across the head when I tried to wrestle his harmonica from him that he was playing three notes on, up, down, up. Then he pulled my platinum hair and started to cry when I smacked him accidentally on purpose on the wrist. I wondered about the etiquette of battering someone else's children. It was a relief to be dropped off in Tallaght, the second most dangerous place in Ireland.

Laura always says that the best way to get over one man is to take up with another one. And as beauty is only skin deep I decided to get my skin cathiodermied to make it beautiful.

I lay being beautified deciding to change my life.

I had been in a blind rut with Richard.

It was OK.

I could accept it now.

Laura always said he was ratty looking and he toes-in when he walks.

I have never listened to a word Laura said before.

One time, when we were friends, before the sexual chemistry developed, Richard bought himself jeans at college. He took them in himself with baler twine. Then he had the audacity to tell me no man would marry me for my dress sense when he called unexpectedly one day and I was wearing a pink fluffy tracksuit with oven gloves on my feet. He thought they might get carried away by my character though.

There was even a time before I became obsessed with him when I went to discos and no one asked me to dance because they thought he was my boyfriend and he would bash them up if he heard about it. I was so angry about this I remember telling him that I wanted a nine to five husband who would idolise me.

And once he came visiting and our underwear was drying on a clothes-horse and he said, "By your knickers shall I know you." He could say Daisy's were white cotton, mine were black lace and Laura's were red nylon.

And the time I was dieting to fit into a tiny borrowed evening dress for the Agricultural Science Ball in First Year, he found me eating a stick of celery for lunch and said he was taking me to St. Patrick's Mental Hospital. That was an interesting evening. Light-headed with hunger, I had a blank after two glasses of wine in the hotel. I was coming round after dinner and Richard suggested I drink a brandy so I didn't feel full after the feed. It went straight to my head again so I missed Laura falling on top of Professor Doyle and Doctor Campion tripping over Mick of The Shovel-Like Hands who had collapsed beneath a table.

I do remember dancing with Richard who asked me first if my dress had been shrunk onto me, and then, assuming I was so pissed I couldn't hear him, he said, "Helen, you are the only woman in the world I can relax with."

I remember hearing him as if through a heavy cloud. And not really listening because I wasn't really interested. He was just an Agricultural Student who fixed his trousers with baler twine.

But I wasn't so pissed that I couldn't shift Pedro the Spaniard at a night-club on Leeson Street afterwards.

Richard always hated me being smarter than him. The day I applied for a job with Guinness he warned me that men don't want brilliant minds that ignore them. He said being a wife and mother was a career too. I was in love with him by then and thought it was his way of proposing. I had only wanted to work there because I'd heard you got a free pint every day. Not even my home-made wine production hobby was enough to persuade them to take me, though. I didn't try to get any other clever jobs after that.

I am a creature of habit. I eat the same brand of cereal out of the same cereal plate every morning with the same spoon. I go for a walk in the same direction at the same time every day. I listen to the same tape on the tape player every morning. I even wake at the same time and say my prayers in the same order every night. (I always pray for myself first in case I am too tired to make them a whole session.)

Richard was just another habit.

Now I am going to get my act together. I am a scientist, an economist, an environmentalist, a blonde. It took five years to make me an Agricultural Scientist at UCD. Waiting for Richard Knight to want me was a waste of academic and personal development.

Instead of choosing marriage I will choose to be a career girl. I am already the Assistant to an Assistant. In a few years with a lot of grovelling and some clawing I may be worthy of Assistant. I will dress for career advancement. No ladders in my tights and nothing in diamanté or rhinestones. I will get my legs waxed, my eyebrows tinted, take up aerobics or squash or some other upwardly mobile sport. I will cycle to and from work.

Of course I might get a company car at the Wild West.

CHAPTER TWENTY-SEVEN

I phoned through to The Assistant of the Wild West, Jason (pronounced Jison) McAuley.

"Are you busy, Jison?" I asked politely.

"I am always busy, dear," said the little pipsqueak. He must have thought he was being facetious, indeed he even uttered a few hollow laughs afterwards. But you are only superior once with me and I clam up forever. "Dear" indeed.

"I would like to speak to you," I said firmly, using my "house-training the pup" voice "about the sheep photographs."

I remained firm and unfriendly throughout the interview which took a damned sight longer than the sheep question because the Big Chief, via Jison, has been analysing how he can exploit my writing talents to their fullest potential. Neurotically, I am convinced now that, but for my questionable and mediocre knack of writing press releases, I would never have got the job.

If my style suits his requirements (and if it doesn't it's no reflection on my writing abilities, and what would he know about writing?) the Big Chief may want me to write Wild West Legends.

Everyone approaches Jison, The Assistant, with a formal scraping approach. If Jison tells me to jump, shall I ask, "How high?"

My sheep are to be used in a promotional photograph for the

Wild West. Dressed as a Red Indian I am to replace a Sick Leave Indian and drive the flock towards the OK Corral for the benefit of a European funded camera.

"Jison," I said during the interview, "in none of the records or research have I read of Indians tending Jacob sheep." But of course Jison wouldn't listen to the lowly Assistant to an Assistant, Management Monkey like me.

"And Jison," I added, "the sheep won't walk towards the camera just because you want them to."

Theirs not to make reply,

Theirs not to reason why,

Theirs but to do and die.

The European Fund photographer arrived; Jacob ewes were set loose in Toomestone. I placed the black plaited wig on my platinum head. Jison arrived to do a bit of PR because the Big Chief was busy doing something important.

The second Jison turned his back, the maddest of the Jacob ewes leapt the gooseberry bushes in front of Doc Holiday's surgery (were there gooseberry bushes in Toomestone?) taking half the sheep-like (no pun intended) flock with her.

Jison was trampled in the ensuing chase and I was stung to bits with nettles as the dirty tarts headed for the swamp-land at the far side of the Wild West.

Cleverly I said, "I told you so, Jison," as I bounded barefoot past him to catch them. Probably I should have picked him up and dusted down his sweet little suit and apologised for being right. And said something like, "We'll leave them alone and they'll come home wagging their tails behind them."

When I reached him, Christopher, the European Fund photographer, was swimming through the swamp to save the life of a ewe lamb who ungratefully made a run for it once she was out. Christopher had cheerfully resigned himself to "losing the light" and was now taking a farming interest in the sheep because he had just bought thirteen acres and was thinking of growing Rare Breeds on them. The other two Indians had skulked off, Indian-like. My feet were black and my toenails rotting and my Indian dress transparently wet by the time I had captured the prodigal lamb (the little git had lain down flat and played dead and I'd had to carry it home).

To think I had taken half an hour this morning deciding what to wear and Aunt Ruby knocking on the bedroom door to tell me she had put the milk in my Sugar Puffs (I hate Sugar Puffs) and they were getting soggy. It had been raining, I thought I would look silly in my summer wardrobe, all my winter clothes were at home in Derryrose.

How convenient that I was presented with an Indian dress on arrival.

Christopher said the best sheep picture he had ever seen was of a naked girl surrounded by sheep, but I thought I would make a more picturesque Indian driving sheep down the Scenic Route. The sheep were there, the scenery, the atmosphere, it had stopped raining – we were all set. Christopher was shouting encouragingly, "The camera loves you, Helen," when a yokel suddenly jumped out from behind a bush and began yelling obscenities and shaking his fist. I wasn't sure what his problem was – it seemed to focus on the fact that we were trespassing on his Right of Way – but he wasn't even angry, just noisy. I fixed my wig and switched on the crocodile tears and grovelled in my nicest voice. God love him, I thought, I must be kind to people less fortunate than myself. Would he ever get the chance to be photographed dressed as an Indian brave?

Under Christopher's direction I started to climb to the top of the Scenic Route, but by the time I had got there, blowing, on my hands and knees, the sheep had scattered to the four winds and no matter how diligently I tried to follow Christopher's instructions (yelled from behind), I couldn't gallop after them without the risk of falling off the edge. Now I understand the intricacies of a fashion shoot and the mentality of the models involved. And the photographers.

I was having a hard enough time climbing the scenic precipice and looking beautiful and not putting my eye out with my pigtail. Christopher (he called me Hell, I called him Christ) followed me closely, hung with cameras, light meters and a mobile phone.

Eventually he was satisfied. He had me looking pretty and wet and pretty wet and he had three blobs of white on the horizon. I took him back to Aunt Ruby's and made him a cup of tea (Aunt Ruby was playing bowls with her church group). He asked me some more questions about Finn Dorset ewes (which I had advised him to stock his thirteen acres with) and roared off in his hired car to the European Fund.

"All's well that ends well," I thought, emptying the teapot and wondering if I had the nerve to return to the Wild West and pick up my handbag. The decision was purely technical. It was almost eight o'clock. Not even the Company Spy would still be there.

"Aunt Ruby?" I asked that evening, as I worried down some tinned rice to please her even though milk puddings make me sick. I am the only Gordon ever sent out to school without a Ready Brek glow.

"Aunt Ruby, I cannot comprehend the concept of nine to five employment. Why, if my work is finished at four o'clock, or at lunch time, can I not just come home? Why must I begin at nine am, with the Company Spy checking that I'm in at nine am, then fill in the next eight hours as fruitfully, or at least as fully as possible? And why if I work till eight o'clock one night can I not take the next morning off?"

I was convinced my career was over, the Big Chief via Jison was going to sack me for incompetence and time wasting, there was no harm in talking a little heresy.

Aunt Ruby was so sympathetic she offered me a drink.

"I sent Mervyn into Coleraine to get me a bottle of Bristol Cream Sherry for my birthday," she complained, "and he brought me home a bottle of fizzy white wine. I know he bought it from a bargain bin. Just because Mervyn doesn't drink it doesn't mean he has to punish me. Would you take a drink yourself, Helen?"

"I would," I said, my tongue hanging out.

"Everyone knows," said Aunt Ruby, "that I will only drink brandy or sherry, and maybe port or a wee martini. I never drink whiskey – well maybe a tablespoon for my health..."

She thinks she will give the wine to Sandra to wet the baby's head.

"Sandra doesn't drink," I said as she poured us a couple of real drinks.

"She doesn't drink because she's an alcoholic," said Aunt Ruby wickedly, "I think that being sober and diligent makes the evening very long, but it does give the conscience a self-righteous feeling afterwards."

"A bit like work," I said, "I would bring in a novel to read, or scribble at stories under the desk if I had the nerve. But I'm a coward. I'm afraid of getting caught."

That night I had an incredibly long and convoluted dream where Christopher held my pigtail and we sang the opera with

"Your tiny hand is frozen" (La Bohème) in it. I was getting hot and cold flushes but that could have been fear about being sacked.

Jison didn't beat about the bush the next morning. My black pig gave birth yesterday while I was running the country (literally). Jison wanted me to photograph the babies, perhaps the shots could be used in the promotional brochure?

So I tried to take a photograph to please him but the inside of the sty was dark and the Lone Ranger, who was watching but not helping, convinced me the sow was as fierce as a crocodile. His brother was a vet in England and one of his pig farmers went into a sty to feed his sows and slipped. The sows attacked him and killed him and ate him.

Always the gullible coward, I tried to take the photograph from a safe distance with the Lone Ranger blocking my line of vision and scaring the life out of me saying she was ready to attack. I asked him nicely a couple of times to move but he's deaf in both ears and couldn't hear me.

By Thursday the killer sow had developed cannibalistic tendencies and had savaged most of her litter. I longed to be a halfwit in such circumstances and sweep the savagery under the cobbles. Go home at five o'clock with the Lone Ranger and not come back.

But that was too simple. We Gordons are bred to No Surrender. The vet came to tranquillise the naughty sow, the massacre was neatly disposed of and by eight o'clock I was back with Aunt Ruby drinking Scotch as if my life depended on it and threatening to roast the black sow at the next Campfire Barbecue.

I had nearly enough overtime done to merit next Monday off. Daisy wants me fitted for a bridesmaid dress now she is nearly sure she wants to marry Johnboy. The Jackson clan took her to The Cobbled Courtyard Carvery on Wednesday night. Daisy said she comfort-ate like a pregnant pig because Jackson dinners are so boring. Too much good taste and good manners and not enough wine.

Daisy thinks Sarah and I should look more sexy than bridesmaid-like which is a very generous gesture because the bridesmaids should never outshine the bride.

So we are being fitted for slinky green velvet halter-neck dresses slit to the navel and bare to the base of the spine. We are having them made in Dublin and we are paying for them ourselves. Daisy has promised not to get married until the Sales so we can buy our green shoes cheap. Mummy says you can buy green shoes in Wellworths for £8.99, and we are snobs to think anyone will ever notice.

The first time we went for a fitting I was taken into the changing room to have my cleavage measured (and padded cups sewn into the dress). Daisy says Sarah nearly threw a wobbly because she thought I was taking my bra off. Sarah didn't even have to be measured because she is a perfect size 10.

Aunt Ruby had gone to play bowls so I phoned Derryrose and told Daisy to organise another fitting for Monday. Daisy agreed, provided it was still raining. There has been torrential rain since the day I joined the Wild West and a forage harvester couldn't make it into a silage field without water-skis.

I phoned through to Jison next morning.

"Are you busy, Jison?" I asked politely.

"I'm always busy, dear," he said rudely, but so convinced I was of a day off that I persevered.

"I have worked six hours overtime this week," I said, "can I take Monday off in lieu?"

On reflection, I think I should just have told him, not asked him. Or taken the day off and pretended I was sick. But then I would have been sick with nerves in case I was caught.

There was a long silence. Then Jison spoke, painfully, as if explaining to an idiot, "Professional staff don't get overtime, Ms Gordon," he said.

And then people wonder at the extent of absenteeism in the workforce.

Chapter Twenty-Eight

On Friday night I collapsed into Derryrose. I swear Jison lay awake all last night thinking of ways to keep me busy. We met by the photocopier this morning. There was egg on his tie.

"The Lone Ranger," he said, "I haven't seen him giving pony-rides this week."

"The rain," I said, "it's jumping six inches off the road, Jison."

"Get that horse out," yelled Jison, making his face turn an unflattering shade of mauve. So obediently I went out in the rain to find the Lone Ranger. And tell him to lead Silver up and down in front of Jison's office until their legs were bleeding, all six of them. The elusive Lone Ranger couldn't be tracked down. I walked round and round the Wild West till I was dizzy. Eventually I found him asleep under a hedge.

"Get off your ass," I screamed, "and do some work!" I sounded just like Mummy asking one of us to wash the dishes for her at home. The Lone Ranger jumped up as if he was shot and raced off in the direction of the pony. So Elisabeth is right after all. Men are more easily bullied than women.

Daddy isn't speaking to Mummy this weekend. Mummy threw his toothbrush in the bin because she said it was causing a bad smell in the bathroom of the brown and white bungalow. Daddy says it was the only AIDS-free toothbrush in Derryrose.

Mummy isn't speaking to Daddy because the fireworks he

organised to raise funds for the Orange Lodge killed Trevvie the Killer Rooster with shock. Trevvie was the best guard dog we ever had. More than Trevvie suffered heart tremors the night of the fireworks. Even Mummy admits to having a few shaky minutes before she remembered it wasn't time for the Second Coming and got back off her knees. She is threatening to write a letter of complaint to the Orange Lodge and sue Daddy.

Daddy has been very subdued all week because he was at a Free Presbyterian funeral on Wednesday and got two hours of Hell and Damnation.

Daisy says she was up the whole night of the fireworks with Bunty who howled steadily with fright. She is going to write a letter of complaint and pretend she is the USPCA.

But it didn't stop Daisy and Johnboy going to Belfast to put a deposit on an engagement ring. Daisy bought her Going Away Outfit in the sales when she was there. I wish her the best with the linen wrap-over skirt and waistcoat. If she doesn't wear it – sure she can keep potatoes in it.

She bought the most perfect bridesmaid shoes for Sarah and me. Swanky "cut the eyes out of a snail" green suede strappy ones with a two inch stiletto heel for half price. The left foot of each has faded to a different shade to that of the right but Daisy bought them anyway. She says no one will notice. If the ground is soft when we are being photographed Sarah and I will be pictured lopsided as we lodge in the soil.

I sucked up to Sandra and she took us to Dublin in the BMW. I even boiled her a couple of duck eggs to eat when we stopped for a picnic. Sandra wants to buy some designer maternity wear. I must make sure I get pregnant in the summertime so I can wear them next.

My bridesmaid dress is tighter than the first day I was fitted.

The dressmaker says if Aunt Ruby feeds me any more rice puddings I may not need the breast pads in my dress. And of course, she added encouragingly, breast size fluctuates at different times of the month.

We decided on printed organza stoles, we thought gloves would be a bit fussy. No, Sarah and I would not feel cold with bare backs, yes I could invest in some fake tan so the colour of my back matched Sarah's.

Ad nauseam. Before we left for home Daisy bought a "Sorry" cake in Brown Thomas for me to give to her because I complained so much about walking to every fabric shop in Dublin looking for printed organza. And not enough time to browse in the second hand bookshops. By the end of it I didn't want to be a bridesmaid any more.

"Hi," said the Lone Ranger on Monday morning. He had burst aggressively into the office at 9.06 am. I had been trying to write my diary and not get caught and my heart nearly stopped with fright. The Lone Ranger reports to me on the hour now with an account of what he's been up to.

"Hi," the Lone Ranger repeated, "Silver is lame." (I won't bother including the expletives, it would take too long.)

It is beyond my comprehension why the Wild West animals are dropping round me like flies. Two sheep and three Indians are Absent Without Leave since last Monday. So much for "Leave them alone and they'll come home wagging their tails behind them". I don't treat the animals badly but as I'm not an animal lover I don't talk to them either. The Lone Ranger says any decent Assistant to an Assistant would have sat up the whole night with a pigging sow. If the sow had eaten me it would all have been in the line of duty. There are more Animal Welfare experts in the Wild West *per capita* than in the rest of the world. I would be lost without the Lone Ranger to advise me.

"And I won't be able to report to you at ten o'clock because I have to have my tea-break."

"Have the Indians come back today?" I asked him but he had decided he was deaf again and didn't answer me.

So I took the Wild West van into Coleraine to fetch emergency rations and miracle medicine for the horse. Soon he will be "Hey Ho Silver, Away."

I did my shopping in Wellworths while I was there. I won't do it again. I felt so guilty about getting caught I peeked around each corner before wheeling the trolley that direction. When I got to the checkout there was an endless queue and neurotically I snapped, "I can't waste my life here," and ran out of the shop, minus the shopping. I must endure Sugar Puffs and rice pudding a bit longer.

When I got home Aunt Ruby had a pot of soup stewing on the range. Aunt Ruby says there are two pots should never be off the stove, one for porridge and one for soup. I often wonder about how fat Mervyn is. Aunt Ruby said, "Did you go back to the Wild West before you came home?"

"Why?" I asked defensively, feeling sick, convinced I had been spotted with the shopping trolley.

But she says a Richard Knight was phoning for me.

I can hardly see Richard in my head anymore – but I can remember us having tea in Bewley's in George's Street once and his hair was greasy and he was wearing a blue sweater darned with green wool. Such a pleasant memory.

I don't need Richard to be a successful Assistant to an Assistant. All this talent. I would have wasted it with Richard. I wouldn't even have written my novel *Chain Reaction* if he had come to see me the time I was dying of a brain haemorrhage. Laura says it's the only honourable thing he ever did.

I think now I am willing to kill myself working to earn so much money I don't have to wear other people's cast-offs ever again.

I might as well keep working. At the minute I have absolutely nothing left to look forward to.

Apart from Daisy's wedding of course. Mummy phoned at 6.01 p.m. to inform me The Ring Went On Today. Johnboy hasn't told his Mummy yet. Then she rang off quickly because she was *en route* to the sunbed. The date is set for a fortnight hence. Daisy is getting married in the Church of Ireland because in Laura's Presbyterian wedding photographs she is pictured signing the register in front of a wall with a damp patch on it. It might have been the photographer's fault, but Daisy isn't going to risk it. It poured the day Laura got married and all the photographs were taken indoors. In front of a stack of chairs.

We are having a really, really coarse hen party this weekend. I am a bit cynical about Daisy's definition of "coarse".

Next morning I was sitting on the radiator in my office reading about the number of fleas Laura Ingalls would have endured in her *Little House On The Prairie*, and Richard phoned.

He says himself and Elisabeth have just received an invitation to Daisy's wedding and is it a joke?

"No," I said, insulted, "why would it be a joke?"

Richard doesn't want to come to the wedding. He says it's too far to drive and they would have to stay overnight in a hotel, and he supposed he would have to buy Daisy a present.

Elisabeth says Richard has 1500 acres but his penny-pinching habits are legendary. In his flat in Dublin he used to hang his hand-washed clothes over the radiator to dry but never turned the radiator on. He once calculated how much it cost to boil the kettle. "The Millionaire," we used to call him.

"Richard," I said, "go to Hell."

And I put the telephone down on him.

A memo arrived on my desk this morning threatening the most severe disciplinary action if employees at the Wild West were caught using Wild West telephones for personal use. I am convinced the lines are bugged.

I had hardly resumed my perch on the radiator when Daisy phoned. She wanted to tell me that though she has learned to love her voluptuous, curvy, and sexy body, she thinks her home-made wedding dress is a bit tight across the bust.

I could do with what Daisy can spare.

"Sew a pile of ruffles on it, Daisy," I suggested flippantly.

Daisy can talk about nothing but the hen party this weekend. She has bought a pile of Christmas decorations in the sales and is festooning the house with them. There will be Christmas lights once she has got them to work. And she has bought a couple of Erotic Literature novels and we are going to read bits out of them to each other.

"Daisy," I said, "you know Sarah and Sandra will find that sort of filth offensive. You know they consider Erotic Literature to be Pornography."

If Jison was listening his ears were probably burning.

Daisy told me I was becoming a dry shite. She says that in Literature, as in Real Life, suggestiveness is more sexy than the full frontal. Keep him wanting more. Let him undress you with his eyes. Don't just run at him naked.

She has already read some extracts to Mummy. Mummy apparently fell about laughing.

I told Daisy to keep her voice down. It was still a fortnight to her wedding.

Daisy roared into the phone, "When you come home at the weekend, Helen, Mummy and I are going to tell you something about goldfish that you never learned at college."

Jison phoned me. "Are you busy, Helen?" he asked politely.

"I'm always busy, Jison," I said politely back again, "but I can always find time for you."

Was I too severely disciplined? And what did Severe Disciplining entail in the Wild West? They could hardly hang me for talking to Daisy and Richard on the telephone.

At primary school once I was severely disciplined when Anto the Medical Doctor showed me his new orange knickers in class. I had to write, "Speech is silver, but silence is golden," one hundred times. Anto wasn't punished.

Jison better not cut up rough with me, I thought, aggressively screwing the lid on my fountain pen. I was not an Assistant to an Assistant to be easily manipulated. I did a Personality Test once at college and they told me I was assertive and self-confident and did not care for the opinions of others. They said that I must be incredibly adaptable to fit so well into a society where I was so unique. Now that I think of it they also told me I had an abnormally high interest in members of the opposite sex.

I rapped Jison's door and, imitating the actions of the Lone Ranger, barged in, ready for a row. If he mentioned personal phone calls I was going to say, "Dock my wages, Jison, sack me if you must, but don't waste my time telling me off like a naughty child."

"Well, Jison?" I enquired politely, formally and professionally, "what can I do for you?"

But he only wanted me to write a press release about the sheep photographs.

Chapter Twenty-Nine

Everyone wrote their own piece of erotic literature for the hen party. Sandra and Sarah weren't sure they wanted to play but Mummy and Ruth Paisley were delighted with the chosen hero – "Very tall, a massive nose and a beard like Abraham Lincoln."

Mummy had invited herself and Ruth because she said she was desperate for a laugh.

This morning she tried to fix the Christmas lights for Daisy. At Christmas she thought she was pulling a fly one. Most people pack away their Christmas lights working and by the next year they are broken. Mummy packed hers away broken and they stayed that way.

Then she and Daddy had a row about the chain-saw which has gone walkabout.

"I suppose Daddy threw it at his arse?" I asked.

"That was just what I said," said Mummy.

"Did you hide it?" I asked.

"That's just what he said," said Mummy.

She was suffering claustrophobic family clutches so Daisy and I took her to the swimming pool and I tried to do twenty lengths proper breaststroke chanting, "I must, I must, improve my bust."

It didn't work and I think I pulled every muscle in my upper arms.

Mummy got bored waiting for Daisy to complete her marathon. She paddled over to her, grabbed her and almost drowned her insisting it was time to get home.

Then she drove out in front of a police Land Rover at the barracks in her haste to get to the bungalow and read *Awakenings*, a trashy novel, for the rest of the afternoon. She said it was to give her ideas for the hen party.

Daisy and I often wonder how Mummy swims – she is under the water more times than she is above.

Daisy shopped and cleaned for the hen party all day Saturday. While cleaning she pulled a curtain down, broke an ornament, fused the electricity, and spilt a saucepan of Weight Watchers soup over the floor because the handle was loose.

In Wellworths she stood in a queue for weighing vegetables because she thought it was the checkout. At the checkout she realised she had forgotten to weigh the bananas. Then she couldn't find her purse to pay for the bits which were weighed. When she finally got back from the scales she put the bananas into someone else's shopping bag.

I made her take me for a cup of tea because the excitement had made me dizzy and she paid for it with five pences.

Daisy has eaten nine rounds of toast today because she thinks she is dieting. She used to weigh a stone lighter, and she swears her eyes were darker, her skin was clearer, her hair brighter and her mouth more sensual. So she has been praying for a bout of food poisoning before the wedding to clean her out. Daisy lives to eat. I eat to live.

I was happily soaking in the bath, listening to Chopin, and about to read *The Complete Book of Insults* as inspiration for the erotic literature evening, when, quite unprepared for it, my world collapsed in round me.

Daisy, her hands covering her eyes, came in to clock on the toilet and to tell me the bells don't ring for her when she and Johnboy embrace, but she has decided that the peace and security she feels with him are enough to last a lifetime. Mummy told her she spent her life in a world of imagination because she suffers an inferiority complex. Mummy says a couple of weeks of married life will cure her of the heart-breaking first love she suffered with Charlie Montgomery. Charlie will fade to a feeling of warmth and affection.

Then she stopped rambling, pulled her trousers up and informed me that Daddy had given her Derryrose as a wedding present.

"That's nice," I said bravely, "I have been thinking of getting a place of my own anyway. Aunt Ruby is cramping my style. She is knitting me a granny-jumper and if I continue living with her I might even have to wear it."

I resolved to drink myself silly at the hen party. The next thing I read in the *Insult* book was a quote by Noel Coward, "Never trust a man with short legs, brains too near his bottom."

Ruth arrived early, Ruth the Trollop of the Town, with chipped nail varnish and dressed to kill in a pair of shorts that left little to the imagination.

"My Sid is going to kill me if he sees me in shorts," she screeched. Ruth never talks, she always screeches. Mummy says she wins the Ugly Witch contest every time by a short haircut.

Elisabeth took the train from Dublin. She says Richard acted like he was in love with her today. He fixed her earring with a pair of pliers and carried her case to the train and said he was leaving immediately in case he cried. The train carriage was invaded by four Dubliners who were doing a medical for the

British Army and lent her their *Now That's What I Call Music 7* tape for her Walkman. They carried her case to the bus station.

"Helen," she said, "you are always the same when I meet you, you never change."

This was meant as a compliment. I advised her to keep a tight hold of Richard even if they fought so much she wanted to run out onto the Naas Dual Carriageway and beg a lorry to run over her.

"All that money," I said, "you would be a fool to let him go – he could buy you a video and everything."

Jennifer also travelled to Derryrose by bus, on the edge of a seat she shared with two of the most pungent little boys she had ever smelt. Jennifer never won any "Cleanliness is next to Godliness" prizes herself at Sunday School. The boys giggled hopelessly when she first sat down beside them but soon got bored and began to arm wrestle. Before Jennifer had a chance to complain, the cavalier adult behind leant forward and charmingly told the boys to "fuckin' quit it, before he fuckin' broke their necks". They obligingly went to sleep after that.

Jennifer says that though some children are sensitive and require gentle guidance, some are born bad and only understand the language of the gutter. Now she is pregnant again she considers herself an expert on child rearing.

Elisabeth tried to find the pregnancy news highly amusing. Jennifer said afterwards it was an overdone sort of joviality that was obviously unnatural. Jennifer, familiar from childhood with the language of the gutter, composed a very blush-making piece of erotic literature.

Which was more than could be said for the hen, who seemed to confuse "erotic" with "romantic" and wrote a ghastly story about being in a car accident with her lover and him screaming for her and dying in her arms in the mangled car. Artistically bruised around the head and ribs, the heroine is so distraught she loses a stone of weight.

The most raunchy thing Sandra wrote was, "He had eyes that could get a girl into trouble and she was a thankless wreck in his arms."

Now that Sandra the Sow is in the family way she drives her husband's BMW and thinks the little Fiesta small. She has offered me it for keeps. I know I should be eternally grateful for such a generous donation to the Helen Gordon Sanity Fund but why does it have to be a Fiesta, a poof's car? Even if I couldn't afford to insure it, I'd far rather drive something flash. How will I ever attract men driving a Fiesta?

"Sandra," I said, genuine tears welling.

Oh, nasty, nasty, I thought much later, I think I'm having my first Derryrose hangover. I should never have mixed my wine with soda water. There was a headache across my temples, my tummy was swollen out like a poisoned pup and I was throwing up wine into the bathroom sink. If I hadn't offered Laura Of The Mammoth Snores a bed share I might have slept the sickness off. When poked she rolls over and stops, but then she rolls back and starts again.

This is terrible and gruesome and naughty, I decided at 4.32 am. I should never have drunk that Spanish wine of Ruth Paisley's. Ruth says she had a bottle of it last night and she danced round lamp-posts, played in a sand-pit, kissed walls, fell down stairs, and knocked over a motorbike. Because she went to the doctor complaining of tiredness and a growth and afraid that she had stomach cancer, Anto the Medical Doctor discovered she was pregnant. Unlike normal middle-aged women, Ruth did not take to her bed. She hasn't stopped partying since. I might voluntarily pay Anto a visit myself. Mummy thinks I'm anaemic I'm so tired all the time. She thinks I should take the week of Daisy's wedding off on the sick.

This is all bloody Daisy's fault, I decide. Why does she have to get married and upset the balance? On the way home from Grubb's pub earlier she told me I was her best buddy. At Laura's hen party Laura told me the same thing. She was drunk too.

I went through my stage of alcohol abuse at university years ago when I was growing up and changing, and I wasn't able to cope with it. With some people, growing up is a simple progression, with me it had been traumatic. Richard had advised me to drink my way through it. He said if I stopped drinking I might use something even worse as a crutch. He probably meant himself. Richard always thought an act of kindness was a sign of weakness, and he is so mean he never sends me a Christmas card.

One time we were queuing to have photographs taken for our student cards and I asked him if my hair was sitting nicely and he said, "I've seen it looking worse," which was the closest he ever got to giving me a compliment.

Laura always says sexiness is to do with personality and that's why some people find Jennifer's simmering aggression sexy and others are attracted to weak, cold people like Richard. Richard wouldn't let me sleep over in his flat once, when I locked myself out of Palmerston Road because it would have compromised his reputation, he said. Note that it was his reputation, not mine, which concerned him.

Once he offered me a sweet and it was such an event I wrote about it in my diary.

And he used to have a code of Protestant ethics at university and I loved him so much I obeyed them.

Always take the stairs, never the lift.

Always work to the end of a chemistry practical.

Attend all nine o'clock lectures.

Be racist and superior and faintly condescending at all times.

Don't own a calculator, borrow one.

Men never wear white socks, gold jewellery, or denim ackets.

Buy your wife a microwave for a wedding present.

Mummy says the aristocrat will bed you but not wed you. It's an awful thing to be so deceived by sentiment and passion. We vill be strangers the next time we meet.

Chapter Thirty

I took the first house listed in the newspaper. It stands on the Nun's Walk in Portstewart and the Irish Sea crashes ten feet from my bedroom.

Mummy wasn't keen. Apart from the obvious concerns about drowning, she thinks rapists will be able to prise open the sash windows. And the other girls are probably drug-taking promiscuous baggages.

"Do you think you are from Buckingham Palace?" I laughed and reminded her that I had been a drug-taking promiscuous baggage in Dublin. She sniffed. I never told Mummy that when the other girls were interviewing me they wanted to know if I made noises making love. I told them I howled like a hound-dog and they said I could move in immediately.

Mummy just doesn't want me to leave home.

"Mummy," I said serenely, "you let Daddy give Derryrose to Daisy," and she started to cry because she says if I'm gone she will have no one left to fight with.

"Shit," I said, "you have Sarah."

Sarah is moving into the brown and white bungalow until something more suitable can be arranged. Mummy had no choice. Sarah threatened to squat in Derryrose otherwise. And Mummy has always been the first to insist that couples need their own space.

"What was that my educated daughter said?" Mummy blew her nose and stood up.

When Mummy and Daddy married, Gran-Gran was obsessed with being the Mistress of Derryrose. At night she would bang on their bedroom door and shout abuse at Mummy. Mummy told Daddy that if he got out of bed to her she would break his legs.

Mummy swears that when she grows old and senile Sarah will pack her into a Home.

But at least Sarah doesn't bother much with boys. Mummy is terrified that without her restraining presence I will catch a baby or a disease.

"Don't let Sarah bully you," I advised, "when I shared a bedroom with her she wouldn't let me put my sticks of make-up in her make-up basket and they lay on the floor where she threw them until she left."

I am very excited about the Nun's House. I have taken the curtains and the bookcase and the flowery eiderdown from my room in Derryrose. I loathe the flowery eiderdown but it gives the new room a sense of belonging. When I've settled in, Bunty can sleep on it. There is even a fireplace so that Mummy can worry that I might set fire to myself.

"Home is still home," Mummy said, "even if you don't get the red carpet anymore."

Before she went home she gave me the expected speech about changing my knickers and reading my Bible everyday. She says she will make an appointment with Anto the Medical Doctor for me. He can give me a tonic to help me cope with full-time employment. I privately think it was the liver I ate at the weekend. There was a mould growing on it. Because I was so mad for a bit of liver I washed it off under the tap and fried on. Finally she went home and I ate with the dope-smoking tarts.

"The last time Mother was here," said Doctor Molly, "she told me I was an introverted, gullible lesbian. She had me so worried that every time I saw a female body, whether it was in the shower or in a magazine, I could feel myself ogling it. Soon I couldn't look at myself in the mirror without feeling guilty. I started to believe what they said in college about worrying yourself to death."

"What happened?" I asked, "did you rush out and make a pineapple tart of yourself?"

"I was in such doubt, I couldn't. Then Mother phoned to say she thought she might have spoken out of turn, which is the closest she gets to an apology. She thinks that maybe intellectuals all behave like me. It was as well I didn't kill myself at the start."

"And because no one likes to feel left out," said Lesley the Lecturer, "she gave me a lecture because my skirt was too long and I hadn't washed my hair in sixteen days. It was only an experiment to see if my hair would start cleaning itself naturally. I never seem to dress properly to please her. I think myself pretty, but she says I need lessons in choosing flattering and complimentary clothes."

We went out to Caesar's Discotheque. I wore my red dress that makes me look like a common vulgar woman, the two dolls wore leather miniskirts because they subscribe to the theory, "If you've got it, flaunt it". Anto the Medical Doctor was propping up a mushroom with a fizzy orange. I kissed him lavishly when I saw him and he told me he never realised I had so many freckles on my legs. "Who was the screw you were talking to?" Molly asked. I told her Anto drove a Hiace van with a mattress in the back of it for any time he fancied a bit of rumpy pumpy. Anto didn't ask me to dance. He just stood at his mushroom and stared at me gloomily. Before the evening was over I had decided that living in Derryrose was cramping my style. At last I was going to be really happy.

"Jison," I said on Tuesday morning, "please can I have compassionate leave on Friday? My sister is getting married and I need to get my black roots touched up."

Jison smiled. He's not that bad-looking when he smiles. I thought he was going to tell me I had beautiful hair but he only said, "There is no need to inform me of your leisure pursuits, Helen. Friday will be taken from your leave allowance."

"Hi," said the Lone Ranger, when I burst in on his tea break to check up on him, "hi, McAuley says he saw you at Caesar's last night and you were drunk." He offered me a Jaffa Cake.

"Is that why he's wearing such a penis happy head?" I blurted out.

"I think he got a cuddle," the Lone Ranger winked at me, "do you want to have a go on my pony? Clear your head."

Silver and I trotted through the Wild West and down towards the beach. I saw the Indians smoking behind the Saloon Bar. It was too nice a morning to cause a scene. I waved to them and the boldest waved back.

"Oh what a beautiful morning," I squawked as Silver broke into a run. It is never my head that is affected by hangovers. They usually lodge in my stomach, and Silver was shaking me up something awful. It was my own fault for not drinking Andrews Liver Salts before I went to bed.

I spent the rest of the day clutching my desk in a sea-sick state of mind.

"Oh Dr Molly," I moaned unprofessionally when she came home from work, "say the magic words and make me better."

Molly laughed. "Don't be insulting," she said, "I'm not a medical doctor. The magic words are 'I will never drink a glass of Guinness, a cherry Brandy, a Malibu and Pineapple and a Gin and Lucozade together again'."

"Even if it seems like a good idea at the time?"

"Especially if it seems like a good idea at the time."

Things were hectic in Derryrose on Friday. The bride and her maid were having a fist fight. Daisy had covered her entire body in Sarah's fifty pound face pack, to try to clear up her spotty chest and arms for the wedding. Sarah pulled a handful of Daisy's hair out at the front where it couldn't be missed. Daisy bit a piece out of Sarah's ear and it wouldn't stop bleeding.

When Johnboy failed to separate them with a basin of water he had broken the floor brush over Daisy's head.

No one is speaking. Sarah is suffering a festering resentment that Daisy has got both a man and a house. Though she persists as a shining example to Feminism, Sarah has a secret old-fashioned regard for the institution of marriage. She has threatened to tie knots in her hankie during the wedding service so Daisy will be barren.

I told Daisy to take a shovel to bed with her and she would give birth to a boy.

Sandra and Ian Flemming, Derryrose's most famous gospel singers – introducing Foetus Flemming – are singing at the wedding. Daisy, who has been comfort eating with wedding jitters all day, wanted to visit them. The last time the Flemmings did *The Irish Wedding Prayer*, Sandra sang "God *help* this couple on their wedding day," instead of "God *bless*..." So I stopped making vol-au-vents and sandwiches and drove her over to Castle Flemming in the Fiesta. There are enough dog hairs in it now for me not to feel naff.

"Daisy," I said kindly, wrestling an egg and onion sandwich from her hand, "you were complaining about your weight only an hour ago. If you eat any more sandwiches there won't be enough for tomorrow night's do."

"I'm going to get my body wrapped," Daisy announced, "tomorrow morning. Guaranteed to lose six inches all over, if I don't eat or drink anything."

"Maybe I should come with you," I said, "the two dolls and I had a midnight feast before I came home and I have developed a pot belly. I will never fit into my bridesmaid's dress."

"That tinker Sarah," Daisy remembered the bald bit at the front of her head and started to cry. "And Laura says Scarlett spilt raspberryade down the front of her flowergirl's frock and she can't get it washed out."

Suddenly visiting the Flemmings and their wedding singing practice didn't seem like a good idea. I detoured to Grubb's pub and we had a drink instead.

"Mummy will be mad as hell with me," said Daisy, "if she smells drink off my breath. And all those dreadful people coming to give me useless presents. Why did I listen to Johnboy's mother and agree that a wedding list is bad manners? What will I do with all those carriage clocks?"

"Give them away to other people for wedding presents," I advised "what have Richard and Elisabeth given you?"

"A microwave," said Daisy.

"Are you sure you want to go through with it?"

"Ask me tomorrow when it's all over."

I used to like the doctor's surgery when I was a child. There are lots of magazines and Reader's Digest books and always plenty of time to read them.

But this morning I was irritated. I was due at the hairdressers at eleven am to have my platinum bob plaited with daisies.

I had to be home by twelve to do Mummy's make-up or she would do it herself – or worse, not wear any. I think there is nothing uglier looking than a woman not wearing make-up. The female owes it to herself and to society at large.

I was just planning to cancel the appointment – the poisoned liver wasn't playing up that morning – and change my cards to somewhere fast and efficient in Portstewart when Anto the Medical Doctor rang for me.

"I feel sick all the time," I told him, "sort of permanently hungover."

He examined everything that it is legal for a male doctor to examine unsupervised. "I'm probably anaemic," I told him. Doctors must get very irritated with patients who diagnose their own problems. At least they are getting well enough paid to put up with it. Anto asked me the usual medical doctor questions. He was very cold and professional. There was no mention of Monday night at Caesar's. He used to be mad about me.

Once, years ago, he told me he had fallen for me the first time he saw me.

Finally he had finished.

"Well," I said, "have you discovered what it is? Have I caught something dreadful at my new job? Or is it the mouldy liver?"

"Helen," said Anto carefully, his soft boiled eyes were glassy, like a dead fish, "you are pregnant."